DON'T MOVE

JAMES S. MURRAY AND DARREN WEARMOUTH

DON'T MOVE

BLACK
STONE
PUBLISHING

Printed in the United States of America

First edition: 2020
ISBN 978-1-982678-32-6
Fiction / Horror

1 3 5 7 9 10 8 6 4 2

CIP data for this book is available
from the Library of Congress

Blackstone Publishing
31 Mistletoe Rd.
Ashland, OR 97520

www.BlackstonePublishing.com

CHAPTER

ONE

The sun had set on the Meadowlands State Fair. Megan Forrester scanned the dazzling array of lights on the midway's rides, corn dog stands, and shooting galleries. The place was buzzing. Above her, excited screams came from the roller coasters rumbling along their tracks, and pop music blared from multiple speakers, filling the warm September air.

Her phone vibrated in the hip pocket of her jeans.

She resisted the temptation to answer. Constant calls and texts were part of her life as operations director at the Hunts Point Distribution Center, but they could all wait a little while longer. Tonight was all about the two most important people in her life.

To her right, her husband, Mike, and eight-year-old son,

Ethan, sat side by side at a picnic table. They looked a lot alike with their side parts and unbuttoned polo shirts. Even the way they enthusiastically attacked their greasy, sugary churros had a similar rhythm.

Megan smiled to herself. She had kept her promise of giving them an unforgettable night out. Despite her rapidly advancing career at one of the most complex logistical operations in the world, a good work-life balance remained an ironclad priority, to keep her family strong.

This was Forrester family time. No compromises.

Ethan gulped down the last bite and pointed at the swing-chair ride. "Mom, can we go on, please?"

Twenty sets of double chairs whirled around a center pole from chains mounted to the large pink canopy. Multicolored lights flashed on the spinning tower.

The sight of riders flying in circles with their arms in the air gave Megan butterflies. Using her problem-solving skills to untangle countrywide logistical nightmares? No problem. This nausea-inducing ride, on the other hand, was out of the question. She checked her watch. It was already close to her son's bedtime, and it was an hours' drive to their house in Ludlow.

"Please," Ethan pressed. "One last ride."

"We need to get you home, mister."

"Aw, Mom, just one more. Dad?"

Mike glanced up, giving her a resigned smile. "I'll take one for the team," he said. "Besides, there's hardly anyone waiting."

"Okay, okay," she replied with mock sternness. "But this is definitely you two's last ride."

Ethan sprang up from the picnic table, thrilled. Grabbing Mike by the hand, he led him over to the end of the short line.

When they got to the ticket booth, her son rocked up on his tiptoes to meet the required height. He just made the cut. The operator grinned and waved him through. He thrust up his thumb as a roustabout directed them to the last two empty seats.

Megan grabbed a stuffed Minion toy off the table. She'd forgotten to capture the elation on her son's face after winning him the yellow toy earlier. Who knew that landing a Ping-Pong ball in a fishbowl could bring such joy?

Most of the available prizes had looked seriously dated—probably older than Ethan. She wouldn't have been surprised to see a Cabbage Patch bear on display. That was the nature of state fairs, though. Nobody came expecting to win a Tiffany bracelet or a pink Cadillac. It was pure, unpretentious fun, a far cry from the stiff and stuffy boardroom at work.

She headed over to the metal barrier for a better view.

This time, she wouldn't forget to record the look on Ethan's face, to capture a video clip that would join the hundreds already on her MacBook's hard drive. Sure, *Ethan Forrester: The Early Years* wasn't bound for box office glory, though it would get plenty of viewings in the Forrester household for years to come.

Megan dug her phone out of her pocket. She focused the screen on the ride and hit the record button.

Mike pulled down the safety bar. Both he and Ethan glanced across to her with beaming smiles, her son's filled with eager anticipation, her husband's with unabashed pride. These were the moments she lived for. They made everything worthwhile, everything complete.

A carnival worker quickly swept around the riders, giving each bar a quick rattle to see that it was properly secured. He then jogged back to the booth.

Moments later the chairs gradually rose to a height of three stories. The canopy rotated in a counterclockwise direction, picking up speed. Soon, twenty pairs of seats whizzed around to the strains of Belinda Carlisle's "Heaven Is a Place on Earth."

Ethan waved down. Megan shook the stuffed Minion in response.

Such a perfect way to cap off the . . .

Suddenly, a metallic groan rose over the sound of the music. Loud and discordant. Unnatural. Close . . .

The crowd surrounding the ride let out a collective gasp as the world around Megan seemed to stop. She froze. Something unplanned was happening. But what?

A heartbeat later, the answer came. The ride's steel center pole groaned and bent in the middle, lurching several feet to the left. Riders instantly went from being spun horizontally to a diagonal revolution. The chairs whipped dangerously close to the ground on the descent.

In an eyeblink, the shrieks of enjoyment transformed into terrified screams.

The Minion and the cell phone dropped from Megan's hands. The ride's center pole let out a grating screech as it sank farther to the left. The vibration resonated through her trembling body.

No. This couldn't be happening.

Mike and Ethan's chair rocketed past, only a yard from the ground. Her husband had his arm protectively wrapped around their crying son. Their look of wide-eyed terror filled her with dread.

Megan drew in a trembling breath and looked frantically toward the ticket booth. A few people in the crowd screamed at the man inside to stop the ride, but he was already frantically hitting buttons and pulling a lever at his console.

Nothing he tried had any effect.

The chairs continued to rocket past, now dangerously close to the ground and soaring back up, almost vertically, into the clear night sky.

Please, God, no.

The crowd surged away from the barrier, as if sensing what might happen. Parents picked up their kids and sprinted for safety, cutting between the nearby food stands. Shouts and screams drowned out Belinda Carlisle's soprano. The buckled center pole continued its slow tilting, bringing each chair ever closer to a high-speed collision with solid concrete.

A double chair smacked into a mother and child who hadn't moved away from the barrier, striking them with tremendous force. Their bloodied bodies flew and then skidded through the crowd, crashing against the side of the high striker game. A man dropped the oversized mallet and knelt beside them, trying desperately to help them, but it was clear they were gone.

Megan staggered back a few paces, unable to take her eyes off her husband and son. She opened her mouth to scream, but nothing came out.

The next double chair obliterated the ticket booth and sent the operator's arm cartwheeling lazily through the air. Two teenagers in the chair slumped lifelessly over the safety bar as they swung upward for the ride's next deadly revolution.

The operator lay facedown on the floor, spattering the height-restriction sign with rhythmic spurts of blood from the stump of his severed arm.

Mike and Ethan flew past Megan again. Both had their legs raised to avoid the ground. The bottom of their chair scraped the concrete, sending sparks through the gaps in the barrier.

The previous chair had cleared a path for them, and they sailed through the remains of the booth and continued upward.

The pole tilted lower.

"NO!" Megan shouted. "PLEASE, GOD, STOP!"

The noise of the scattering, screaming crowd drowned out her useless plea.

The next set of chairs, containing a mother and daughter, zipped down and hammered head-on into the concrete with a crunching thud. Their knees and faces took the full brunt.

Ethan and Mike rose again to the zenith of the near-vertical revolution. She couldn't process events at the speed they were happening. Couldn't move. Nothing had prepared her to watch the two most precious things—her whole life—seconds from a brutal end.

Another chair slammed down, giving the riders no chance.

Then another.

And another.

Six more people flung against the concrete like bugs against a windshield. At that speed and direct angle of impact, none stood a chance.

Each chair continued at a low angle, flattening small booths that sold caps or cotton candy and mowing down small trees to the right of the ride. Branches caught a corpse and tore him free from the ride, and there he hung, arms loosely at his side, face gone from the earlier impact.

A shriek beside her broke Megan out of her paralysis. She pushed the terror down and searched her mind for a solution. Anything to save her husband and son before their devastating impact with the concrete.

Only three chairs remained on the ride. Six surviving people of the forty who had boarded. They arced through the zenith and plunged downward, with Mike and Ethan's chair at the back of the trio. Behind them, mutilated bodies and parts lay in mangled pieces of wreckage. One woman hung from her seat by a twisted leg, the ragged end of her shinbone gleaming white where it protruded from her yoga pants.

The first of the undamaged chairs battered the ground, slinging blood over the horrified crowd.

A man with a blood-spattered face looked at Megan in terrified bewilderment. She had seen him send his two kids on the ride before Mike and Ethan.

Megan vomited nothing but bile. Tears filled her eyes as she stood alone in front of the ride, taking rapid, shallow breaths. Helpless.

This had to be a nightmare. It couldn't end like this.

She heard a low groan of rending metal.

One of the chains supporting the next pair of seats snapped free from the extreme centrifugal force. A teenage couple gripped the safety bar, yelling as their chair swung wildly to the side. The second chain broke, separating them from the ride entirely.

The freed chair catapulted high over the crowd's heads, through the darkness, and arced down toward the pirate-ship ride. The people disembarking had stopped to watch the disaster playing out from a distance. Now they dived for cover. Some tried to run but got bottlenecked in an exit big enough for only two at a time.

The teenagers' chair smashed into the crowd, knocking people aside like bowling pins before slamming into the hull of the pirate ship.

Megan spun back to face the swing-chair ride as sirens wailed in the distance.

She swallowed hard, and tried to make eye contact with her husband and son. They simply hugged each other, eyes shut tight, as if resigned to their gruesome fate.

A second before Ethan and Mike collided with the ground, the support chains snapped free. Their undamaged chair hurtled outward at a much lower angle, cartwheeling inches over the people's heads. The dangling chains scythed through the scattering people as they fled toward the food stands.

Fairgoers ducked left and right as the chair plummeted toward a burger shack.

The back of Mike and Ethan's seat crashed through the serving window and came to a violent stop on the asphalt.

Megan screamed. She sprinted toward the stand, weaving through the dead and injured. Her new, white sneakers splashed through slicks of blood. She feared the worst as she closed in, praying that they were somehow still alive, the sole survivors of this mechanized slaughter.

Eighteen more seats still rotated around the canopy, most of them carrying disfigured corpses that repeatedly smashed into the concrete.

Chains continued to break free and whip through the air with chilling, decapitating force.

Megan ignored the danger. All she cared about was Mike and Ethan. She reached the burger stand and peered inside. An overhead strip light sparked. Debris littered the little square cook shack. Crumpled plywood. Hot griddles. Napkins. The owner must have fled because the only two people inside were Mike and Ethan. Both lay still, their arms and faces peppered with scratches and small cuts.

Her husband's eyes flickered open. He winced and turned to check on his son.

Ethan also came around, groggy and confused. He burst into tears and hugged his father.

A wave of relief washed over Megan, though she remained acutely aware that this wasn't over until a doctor could confirm the extent of their injuries. But they were alive—probably the only two from the whole ride.

"Thank God," she breathed. "Ethan, it's Mommy. You'll be okay, baby."

Megan ran to the side of the stand, ripped the door open, and stepped inside. A small fire had broken out where the edge of the chair bashed the stove. Only a few wood planks and a stack of frozen patties stood in her way. She stepped around them and raced through the thin smoke.

Ethan held both arms toward her for a tearful embrace.

"One second, baby," she said. "Let's get you both outta here first."

Her husband was in obvious pain. He grunted, clutching his ribs. Likely multiple fractures, making it hard to breathe. Blood trickled from a gash above his temple. She couldn't see any nasty cuts on Ethan, who stared at her with tears welling in his eyes.

She crouched to free the safety bar. It wouldn't budge. The impact had bent it downward, jamming Mike and Ethan into their seats. She scanned the chair at both ends for some kind of button or lever, without success.

Mike tried to help her by wrapping his hands around the bar and heaving upward.

Nothing. The bar would not move.

The crackle of flames in the background grew louder. Smoke billowed, making her eyes water.

Two men appeared at the front window.

"Help us!" Megan yelled. "It's stuck."

Both men recognized the situation and went for the door.

Ethan coughed in the fast-thickening smoke.

"I'm gonna get you out soon, baby," she said, unconvinced by her own words.

Megan untied the sweater from her waist and gently placed it behind her son's head. She wasn't sure how much it would help, but she didn't know what else to do in this moment.

A sudden whoosh of flames erupted to her left. She turned, and smoke burned her throat.

Flaming grease had run from an upended griddle and flowed across the floor, toward the chair. Megan and Mike glanced at each other. The look in her husband's eyes told her that he, too, realized the consequences of not getting out in the next few seconds. Both grabbed the bar and lifted with their combined strength.

Again it didn't move.

"Someone, help us!" Megan shouted. She couldn't hide the looming reality from her son any longer.

Fire licked its way up the walls and across the ceiling. The cheap wooden structure was no match for the flames.

The burning grease reached Mike's and Ethan's feet. They screamed in agony as flames consumed their shoes.

Through the dense smoke, Megan spotted the locking pin, peeking out beside Ethan's elbow. Fire blazed around them, but there was still time. She reached for it.

Flames from the grease fire immediately scorched her arm in 450-degree heat.

The overwhelming pain sent her staggering back. Skin shriveled and bubbled on her forearm. Regardless, she advanced toward her husband and son again, determined not to leave them to this terrible end.

A wall of fire exploded in front of her. Her body betrayed her and instinctively pulled away from the heat. Clutching her seared arm, she fell backward.

She scrambled to her feet but froze, terrified to move any closer to the swing chair.

Frozen by her fear.

Strong arms grabbed her and pulled her back through the kitchen. She fought them with all her strength.

"Get the hell off me!" she yelled.

"You can't stay in here, lady!" a man replied. "It's suicide!"

She struggled again, unable to break free.

Inside the stand, fire consumed the writhing bodies of her husband and son as their screams blended with the roar of the flames. Their hair flared up like lit matches. Then, as their faces blackened and their bodies contorted in the intense heat, the cries mercifully died away.

Now only the sounds of burning wood, the screams of the crowd, and the approaching emergency vehicles filled Megan's ears.

The burly carnival worker who had pulled Megan from the flames finally let her go.

She collapsed to all fours and crawled toward the blazing food stand.

Heat drove her back. She could no longer see inside.

It was all over in less than a minute. Her son's and her husband's lives, her hopes and dreams, replaced by numbness and devastation.

She stared at the roaring fire for a few seconds, then doubled over and vomited.

Her family was gone.

CHAPTER

TWO

Megan sat behind the wheel of her parked Lincoln Naviga-
tor, watching the sun rise over the Bronx. She turned up the
air-conditioning to beat back the already building heat of a
stifling New York summer. Outside, dew glimmered on the
asphalt of the small parking lot. No lights were on inside the
drab single-story brick building of Our Lady of Saints Church.
She was the first to arrive.

This camping trip was Megan's first serious excursion outside
the house since that horrific day last fall. Her first vacation without Mike and Ethan. A positive step that she knew she needed to
take. Once again the sleeping pills hadn't worked, so she had set
out early. It was a choice between leaving the house or giving in to

depression, mentally talking herself into another day of seclusion. Megan was determined to get her life back on track, no matter how hard her inner demons fought to keep her down.

Mike and Ethan would hate to see me like this. Those demons can return to hell.

These thoughts had proved hard to act on. The early morning emptiness of the church reflected her feelings. Ever since that fateful night in New Jersey, nothing had replaced her sense of loss. The gut-wrenching images of her son's and husband's final moments. The long burn scar on her right forearm providing a constant, painful reminder.

And the knowledge that someone had uploaded footage of the disaster onto the internet for all eternity. Some unfeeling ghoul had filmed part of the carnage on a smartphone, capturing the moment Mike and Ethan's chair slammed into the food stand. YouTube had quickly taken it down, but not before less savory sites—untouchable from US soil—had copied the video and posted it, with no regard for her or for any of the other victims' families.

But those bastards wouldn't drag her down.

Megan thought back to how different her life was only nine months ago. Running the day-to-day operations of Hunts Point, the largest food distribution center in the world, was no easy task. She handled the logistics of moving nearly half the meat, produce, and fish in the Northeast each day and oversaw more than two billion dollars in annual sales. The job was a nearly impossible daily puzzle: how to get perishable items into stores and onto people's tables before they expired, any and every way possible. Rail, truck, boat, plane—she oversaw it all. Every day was a different challenge. The job invigorated her, and in such an old-school, male-dominated industry with so many larger-than-life personalities, she had to admit, it felt great to be on top. She had earned her reputation as the ultimate puzzle solver through her intellect, instinct, and logistical skills.

The accident had stripped her of all that. In the space of a moment, it all had ceased to matter.

She had to try to get her life back on track, and today was the first step in that direction.

At seven a.m. sharp, a rust-speckled white bus pulled into the parking lot, belching smoke from its exhaust pipe. It had Our Lady of Saints painted on the side and could probably carry fifteen at a push. She had hardly visited Mike's old church since his funeral. On the rare occasions that she did, Pastor Rizzo had offered a shoulder to cry on and, most recently, a place on the bus for this outing.

Why not? she'd thought back then. It wouldn't be a wild party—it was a church camping trip, after all. Maybe it was just what she needed to ease her way back into society.

The passenger door on the bus rattled open. It was the old folding type. The church was not exactly blessed with money, but she knew they did great work in the community: rehab programs, volunteer work, charity events. The small congregation pulled its weight despite the lack of financial resources.

Pastor Rizzo, his white hair matching his shirt and pants, clambered down the steps until his sandals crunched against the gravel. He smiled in the direction of her car. Warm and sincere. The man was genuine, and though she had shunned his offers of regular counseling, she liked and trusted him.

Megan turned off the engine and popped the hatch. Climbed out of the Lincoln and went around to the back.

Rizzo came over. "Good to see you, Megan. Let me help you with those bags."

"It's okay. I've got it."

"You sure?"

"Positive. But thank you."

Grief didn't make her incapable of doing basic tasks. She had fiercely maintained her independence. She needed it to keep herself sane.

"We've got a bunch of good folks coming along," Rizzo said. "Have you met my daughter, Emma, yet?"

"Hmm, I don't think so."

"She'll make you feel part of the group, don't you worry. Are you excited to see West Virginia?"

"For sure," she lied.

Excitement wasn't quite the right word. Maybe *resigned*. Or *resolute*. She had to try to get back some semblance of normality. She was determined to try.

Megan heaved out her backpack and closed the hatch, then hit the lock button. The lights on the SUV blinked.

Rizzo walked with her toward the small bus. "If you ever feel like talking—"

"Honestly, I'm okay. You don't need to worry about me on this trip."

"I'm just saying. No pressure. I'll be here if you need to talk. Besides, a few days camping in a forest is a great way to unwind."

"That's what I'm hoping for."

Megan appreciated his offer to listen, but if she was being honest with herself, talking any more about it was only making things worse. After countless therapy sessions over the past nine months, they were starting to feel as if they did more harm than good. They had an inconvenient way of keeping mental wounds open, the memories fresh and stark. None of it was Pastor Rizzo's fault, of course. She just wanted to enjoy some time in the wilderness, taking in the natural splendor while getting a momentary reprieve from her guilt. From her anger.

You could have done more. What if you had . . .

She stopped herself. This was precisely why she had chosen to go on this trip: to be around other people again and not let herself drown in what-ifs.

A man in his early fifties, dressed like a model from a North Face catalog in his branded boots, hiking pants, and camouflage jacket, opened the side cargo hold of the bus. His slicked-back hair and the strong scent of his cologne seemed at odds with his clothing—and maybe with this trip.

"Hey there, I'm your driver slash semiprofessional wilderness guide, Paul DeLuca. Good to have you on board. Ready for some high adventure?"

She shook his hand. "Megan Forrester. Nice to meet you. Hope you brought a map."

DeLuca laughed and tapped the side of his head. "Young lady, I *am* the map. We'll find out soon enough, won't we?"

She smiled at him. "Yep, after seven hours of driving first . . ."

"Don't forget about the two-hour hike after that to get to the campsite before dark," he added. "Damn, I better review that map after all, huh?" He laughed and loaded her backpack into the compartment.

She liked his sense of humor. Easy and light. Megan turned and boarded the bus.

For whatever reason, Pastor Rizzo followed her inside. She hoped he wouldn't act as her shadow for the entire long weekend.

The temperature inside was the same as outside, making her glad she'd dressed in layers. She slipped off her jacket. This was

shaping up to be a T-shirt kind of day. A faint odor of stale cigarette smoke hung in the air, though an old citrus air freshener
battled it for dominance.

Megan considered her seat selection. She planned to ease
herself into this trip. Sitting on her own, listening, watching,
and getting a read on the rest of the group would be a good start.
She wasn't sure she'd know any of her fellow campers anyway.
She made her way to the rear of the bus and sat on the left side.
The cream upholstery had seen better days, but it appeared clean
at least.

Moments later, a minivan swept past the bus and parked next
to Megan's SUV. An old couple, gray-haired with matching red
waterproof jackets, got out of the front. The woman slid open
the side door, and a young child jumped to the concrete. Possibly around eight years old. Also wearing the same red waterproof
jacket, which she guessed was standard issue in their family. They
grabbed their packs and headed over to DeLuca.

"That's Jim and Maryann, and their grandson, Connor,"
Pastor Rizzo said. "Nice family from Melrose. You'll love some of
Jim's stories about 1960s New York."

"A bit of a character?"

"He's got character to spare."

The grandparents, maybe in their midseventies, moved with
youthful vigor. It appeared to Megan that they had spent a lot of
time outdoors. They loaded their backpacks and a large cooler
into the cargo hold, then boarded the bus.

Rizzo moved along the aisle to greet them. He turned and
introduced Megan. The group exchanged pleasantries, and the
family took seats in the middle of the bus.

The pastor glanced at his watch and gazed toward the road.

They were due to depart in five minutes. Much later, and they'd be hiking through darkness this evening.

Rizzo breathed a sigh of relief when a 1990s Pontiac Firebird entered the parking lot and crunched to a halt in the last parking space. A slim brunette in a pale tracksuit got out on the passenger side. Megan recognized her from a few previous visits to the church. Only in passing, though she assumed this was Rizzo's daughter. A stocky man with a shaved head got out on the driver's side. DeLuca warmly welcomed them, and they loaded their packs and followed him onto the bus.

The couple, perhaps a shade younger than Megan's thirty years, took the front seats. Both carried breakfast meals from McDonald's. Ethan had loved the Happy Meals and always dug straight into the box for the toy.

Stop torturing yourself, Megan.

DeLuca sat behind the wheel.

The bus's engine roared to life.

"Guys," Rizzo said in a raised voice, "this is my daughter, Emma, and her boyfriend, Ryan. You'll all have plenty of time to catch up on our way to West Virginia. Everyone ready for a great weekend?"

A couple of muted yeses.

Awkward.

Rizzo glanced around at the passengers. "Oh, come on. You can do better than that. I said, are we ready to go!?"

This time, everyone, including Megan, murmured a response.

It was perhaps too early to elicit the reply he'd hoped for. Also, the tone of the pastor's question didn't feel quite right, as if they were all children heading to Disney World, rather than a group of adults going on a sedate camping trip. Still, Megan admired his enthusiasm.

"How about we crank up the AC?" DeLuca announced through the address system.

The ceiling fans whirred. Soon, cooler air flooded into the bus, knocking off the warm edge. Megan guessed that at this point, the heat was the least of their worries. The sylvan splendors of West Virginia lay ahead, that is, if they could make it there without breaking down on 78 West first.

Still, she already felt comfortable among this group. So far no one appeared to be a drama queen, waiting to go off at the first hiccup. That suited her and what she needed right now, and she looked forward to an uneventful trip as the bus pulled away.

CHAPTER

THREE

Ricky Vargas walked in front of the parking lot entrance, directly in front of the departing bus, blocking its exit. He had made it despite a raging hangover. One too many shots of tequila last night with the guys. Five hundred smackers down on the poker game too. But this little jaunt into the great outdoors paled all that into insignificance.

A few yards in front of him, the bus juddered to a halt.

Vargas readjusted his grip on the straps of a heavy carryall that he'd slung over his shoulder.

His black leather jacket creaked.

He dropped his smoke on the pavement and crushed it under his boot.

This should be interesting.

Behind the dark windshield, both Pastor Rizzo and the driver got up from their seats. The door rattled open, and they came out to meet him. Surprised by his presence, to be sure. Their faces couldn't conceal the fact that they considered him a monkey wrench in their works. Rizzo gave him an inauthentic smile.

"Yo, Pastor Rizzo," Vargas said. "Got room for one more?"

"Hello, Richard," Rizzo replied, and Vargas heard the defensive edge. "I must say, I'm surprised to see you here. We haven't seen you at Mass in months."

Richard. Only Ricky's mother called him that before she died—and, annoyingly, so did the pastor, ever since Vargas dated his daughter a year ago. Pastor Rizzo hadn't been too keen on the matchup. While dating Emma, Vargas had attended Our Lady of Whatever the Hell to be polite. But he stopped going after she dumped him.

"Been busy," Vargas replied. "You know how it is. Anyway, a ride to the wilderness seemed like a good idea. You know, chill for a bit, lose the Bronx heat for a weekend. That sort of shit."

"You wanna come camping with the *church group?*" DeLuca asked with a hint of disbelief.

"That's right. Don't believe we've had the pleasure. Name's Ricky Vargas. Most people call me Vargas." He shot a look at the pastor.

"I'm Paul DeLuca."

They shook hands. It was like gripping wet lettuce.

"I mean, all are welcome, right, Pastor Rizzo?" Vargas asked. "I mean, that's what the flyer posted in the grocery store said."

"Yes," Rizzo replied. "All our parishioners are welcome, even those who have strayed. And you're sure you want to come?"

"Hundred percent. I love this shit."

The pastor glanced back to the bus. "Okay, but you should know, Emma's here with her new boyfriend."

"New boyfriend. Got it," Vargas replied. "Don't worry, I'm not gonna make any trouble. We'll all be making s'mores by sunset."

"I'm not sure Ryan will see it that way," Pastor Rizzo replied.

Vargas grunted a laugh. "Ryan . . . Andrews? That jacked-up mechanic from Soundview? Ha-ha, don't worry, boss. He won't get any hassle from me."

"I hope not." Rizzo looked puzzled. "Honestly, I never took you for the outdoors type."

"What can I say? Appearances can be deceptive."

"They sure can. It's just that given your . . . colorful past . . ."

"What's all that stuff you say about turning the other cheek?" Vargas asked. "Surely you believe people can change, Pastor Rizzo."

"Yes, of course I do."

"So let me prove it to you. I've done my time; I'm done with all that. Just looking for a break from this hellhole, a break from this life. I thought the church could help me with that. Was I wrong?"

"No, of course not," the pastor replied.

"Good, because the tent I bought isn't refundable. Neither are my Cup O'Noodles."

The pastor and the driver glanced nervously at each other. Vargas could see the gears spinning in their minds, trying to come up with a way to deter him from joining their little expedition. Some excuse to keep their saintly consciences clear. That wasn't happening.

"So? Can I join?"

"Okay, Richard. But I'll warn you right now, any fooling around and you'll have to leave immediately."

Vargas grinned. "That's my man. Right there."

"Just behave," Rizzo pleaded. "We've got a mixed group on the trip, and the last thing we need is anyone causing friction."

"You've got my word, Pastor Rizzo."

The pastor nodded to the driver, who dutifully moved to the side of the bus and opened the luggage compartment. He extended a hand toward Vargas.

"Pass me your bag."

"God helps those who help themselves, right? I got it."

Vargas walked past him, ducked down, and stuffed his large carryall in the far corner. Nobody was touching his gear, just as he wouldn't mess with theirs. He followed Rizzo and DeLuca onto the bus.

Emma stared, openmouthed. Ryan glared at him through narrowed eyes.

"And good morning, everyone," Vargas said.

Emma let out a deep sigh and turned toward the window.

"What's he doing here?" Ryan snapped to Rizzo.

It sounded more like a demand to Ricky. Clearly, Emma's new boyfriend felt at ease calling the shots in the Rizzo household.

"Same as you," Vargas said before the pastor could answer. "We're going camping, right? Now, if you don't mind, I'm gonna catch some z's."

He continued down the aisle before the situation escalated. Ryan Andrews was a pain he didn't need. Yes, Vargas had ripped him off a few years ago. And yes, the guy knew that Vargas used to date his girl. But for now, best to avoid any heat.

A woman sat at the back-left corner of the bus. He thought he recognized her from somewhere, though she looked a little clean-cut to be one of his acquaintances. Prim, wholesome, staid. His polar opposite.

Vargas peeled off his jacket and flopped down on the opposite seat. The cure for his hangover was sleep, and he guessed she wouldn't disturb him.

The woman eyed the ink on his forearms: one of a snake wrapped around a dagger; the other a full sleeve he'd gotten while drunk. In fact, he still didn't know what some of the images were supposed to mean.

"Do I know you?" he asked.

"Sorry?" she replied meekly.

"I'm Ricky."

"Megan."

"You look familiar. Wait, do you work at the restaurant Escape Latino?"

"No. I don't work anywhere at the moment."

"Same here," Ricky replied. "I guess that makes us soul mates."

She smiled cautiously. "If you say so."

The address system crackled. DeLuca came over it saying, "All right, folks. Now that we're on the road, let me give you a bit of information about our trip, starting with the mysterious history of the region."

Vargas groaned. "Jesus Christ."

"Not your thing?" Megan asked.

"I'm not big on listening to the Bronx's answer to Crocodile Hunter."

He leaned back and closed his eyes, hoping the driver wouldn't bullshit for too long. The three hours' sleep he had grabbed before heading to the church just wasn't nearly enough. He consoled himself with the hope that DeLuca's blathering would help him get to dreamland that much sooner.

The quicker I fall asleep, the quicker we get there . . .

CHAPTER

FOUR

Megan sat waiting for bus driver Paul DeLuca's briefing after his grand announcement about their destination. But instead of interesting facts and engaging yarns about the area, all that came through the overhead speaker was sporadic hisses of static interspersed with confused mutterings as the man struggled to formulate a coherent sentence. The knowledge that was supposed to be in their guide's head must have stayed buried in a dark recess of his brain, inaccessible for now. The man had stage fright before an audience of eight.

Sunshine broke through the clouds, brightening the New Jersey landscape. Megan took a pair of sunglasses out of her small backpack and put them on. The bus passed factories, many of them abandoned to rust and ruin, others still putting out smoke and strange smells. But she knew that soon enough, they would get through the industrial wasteland and into greener pastures.

Ricky Vargas had stretched his leather jacket over his head, muffling his snores. He was the only person in the group that Megan felt uncertain about. His looks and attitude just seemed out of whack with everyone else. And his presence had visibly rattled Ryan. She sensed that his joining for the weekend had added an element of drama to what was supposed to be a quiet and relaxing trip.

Megan didn't need that.

But she had learned over the years not to judge on appearance. Moreover, she was in no position to judge anyone, not after she froze at the sight of those flames and backed away from that locking pin. That was far worse than merely stinking of stale tobacco and alcohol and sporting a few tattoos.

The bus pulled into a rest area on I-95, and DeLuca stopped in front of the mini-mart. He sifted through a bunch of papers scrawled with handwritten notes. A few dropped to his side.

Pastor Rizzo scooped them up. "No sweat, Paul. We know you've got this."

"It's just a couple of minor details to get the narrative straight," DeLuca replied sheepishly. "I want to make sure I tell you the right history. But it seems like the wilderness suits me better than being a tour guide."

"We've got faith in you, my friend." Pastor Rizzo smiled. "Take your time."

The older couple whispered to each other, and Megan heard the word "clueless." It was a bit early to judge, though, and that was perhaps unfair. Regardless, the comment was loud enough to reach the driver's seat. And it lacked any kind of subtle filter.

A moment of silence followed.

Megan scanned her phone, gazing at nothing in particular, waiting out the awkward moment.

The bus doors slid open, letting in warm, humid air.

DeLuca peered over his shoulder. "Guys, grab anything you need from the store. Our next stop is Hagerstown."

Emma and Ryan rose from their seats and headed out. As they stepped onto the stairs, Ryan flashed a glance at Vargas. Eyes narrowed, intense and unwelcoming. Emma grabbed his arm and pulled him outside.

Almost as if he had sensed the glare, Vargas pulled the jacket away from his face. He yawned, looking around until he locked eyes with Megan. "We've stopped already?" he asked.

"Quick break. We'll be on the road another four hours."

"Better get my nicotine fix."

Vargas groaned to his feet and headed out. He gently slapped Pastor Rizzo on the back as he passed. A friendly gesture between people who were comfortable with each other, yet his action made Rizzo's posture stiffen.

The pastor waited for Vargas to leave, then headed to the back of the bus. He perched on the seat opposite Megan. "Don't worry about Ricky. He looks intimidating, but he's got a good heart."

"What's the story with him and Ryan?"

"Ricky dated my Emma last year. It didn't end well." Rizzo looked out the window to where Vargas stood smoking a cigarette, facing away from the bus and talking on his cell phone. He stood several yards from the gas pumps but still close enough to cause concern. "He didn't mistreat her. They just weren't a good match. And I'm not sure he can get past his own past."

Megan arched an inquiring eyebrow. "I get that," she said.

"So that's Ryan's beef? I mean, getting off the bus, if looks could kill . . ."

"Well, there's more to the story. I think they had a deal that went wrong. Something to do with custom parts that never showed up to Ryan's auto garage. It cost him about two grand."

"I guess that'd do it. What about Emma?"

Rizzo pursed his lips. "She's forgiven Ricky. We all need to move on at some point."

Megan nodded. This was something she didn't need to be told, though doing it was a lot harder than merely knowing it.

Vargas climbed back on board and headed back to his seat. His large, lean frame filled the aisle, and he stooped to avoid hitting the ceiling. Rizzo headed in the opposite direction, and they awkwardly squeezed past each other.

"What's the old man been telling you?" Vargas asked.

Megan shrugged. "Nothing much."

"Hey, I just realized where I seen you."

The words filled Megan with dread. The footage on the internet, or the news footage of her being led to an ambulance, wrapped in a blanket, tears streaming down her soot-covered face.

She was relieved when he said, "You're actually Supergirl in disguise. Here to save us from the driver and his nonsense lectures."

"That's me."

He let out a chesty laugh. "I'll be sticking with you, Supergirl."

The idea didn't seem all that appealing, though she wasn't too worried. Ricky would tire of her once he realized she wasn't the life of this party. They were complete opposites. Different backgrounds, different ways of existing in the world. Almost certainly different social circles and outlooks on life. That said, she found his upbeat nature mildly infectious.

Ryan and Emma boarded the bus, and the doors closed. This time Ryan went straight to his seat, perhaps under instruction from the pastor's daughter to behave. Megan didn't care as long peace reigned for the trip.

The chances remained slim because of what Pastor Rizzo had told her. Nobody liked getting ripped off, especially if the person ripping you off was your girlfriend's ex.

She would do well to keep her distance. Avoid any flare-ups.

Moments later, the air-conditioning did its job again before the bus had a chance to transform into a hothouse on wheels.

DeLuca navigated out of the gas station, and they hit the road again. Next stop: Maryland, three hours ahead.

A few minutes farther along the highway, the speakers crackled.

Deluca seemed to have found his confidence. "Ladies and gentlemen, now that I've had a moment to review my notes, our destination is the Monongahela National Forest in West Virginia, over 900,000 acres of untouched territory, and I'd like to tell you a bit about the region."

He rattled off a number of facts about the area. It sounded like a list regurgitated from Wikipedia, interspersed with a few lame jokes. Megan knew that the area was a vast wilderness, but she had never visited before.

Vargas leaned over the aisle. "You said the next leg of the trip is three hours?"

"Yep."

"That's gonna seem like three *days* if this dude keeps talking."

Megan shushed him with a half smile. DeLuca was trying his best to be a good tour guide, and she doubted anyone would remember the irrelevant factoids, anyway. She'd done it herself during board meetings at Hunts Point. The important skill was in identifying and retaining the key bits of information. Amid the tide of facts pumping through the speakers, she expected to glean at least a few useful nuggets.

". . . Now for the juicy parts," DeLuca said. "The place I'm taking you is steeped in mystery. A group of two hundred Quakers attempted to establish a settlement here in the early 1800s. Five years later, after nobody had heard from them for some time, a party was sent from Pennsylvania to investigate. All they found was a rotting cart and the word 'burro' carved into a tree. The two hundred Quakers, nowhere to be found."

DeLuca paused, maybe in anticipation of a collective sharp intake of breath that never came.

"And if that's not mysterious enough," he continued, "during the 1930s a few hikers went missing in the very same forest. They were never found. Some say their spirits haunt the woods in the dead of night, begging people for directions to Richmond."

Vargas laughed at that, perhaps a little too loud.

Ryan spun in his seat and eyeballed the big man. Emma grabbed his shoulder and dragged him down. He obviously had a serious axe to grind with Vargas, who seemed utterly unconcerned. Instead, he relaxed back in his seat and drew his jacket over his face again.

"Our mission," DeLuca said in a mock-serious tone, "if you choose to accept it, is to discover the Quaker settlement and unravel the mysteries of nature, all while enjoying the scenic delights of the beautiful national forest. Does anyone have any questions?"

The young boy, Connor, shot up from his seat. "But if this forest is haunted, won't we be in danger?"

The grandparents chuckled. So did Rizzo.

DeLuca laughed. "Trust me, Connor, my scouting skills will keep us safe."

Megan drew in a deep breath. In another time, she could have enjoyed the levity, both fun and dark. Now any talk of danger sent a chill down her spine. It all was still too raw. The passage of time had been no healer.

So far, a simmering feud and an inept tour guide suggested that this trip was going to be a lot rockier than she had envisioned.

But it was a little late to back out now. She would stay out of any conflicts and make of it what she could.

As the thought passed through her head, Ryan sprang up from his chair. He shook free of Emma's grip and stormed toward the back of the bus, staring at Vargas with a directness that could mean only one thing.

Oh, shit.

CHAPTER

FIVE

Megan drew in a deep breath. A fight was coming within seconds, right beside her seat. She had an instant to decide whether to shuffle toward the window and hope the violence didn't spill across the aisle.

Or she could act.

She started to get up, but something told her to stop.

Was it that same quiet voice that had stopped her last-ditch attempt to save her husband and son? She cursed under her breath.

Ryan's tight-fitting T-shirt accentuated his muscular frame. He clearly worked out, and the buzz cut and stubble added to the effect, making him appear as a mean, formidable opponent. Not part of the smiling, happy couple Megan had first seen in the parking lot.

That said, the man he was approaching didn't look like anyone to mess with.

Do something, Megan.

But her body's response was simply butterflies in her stomach. And paralysis.

Ryan reached over the opposite seat and ripped Vargas's leather jacket off his face. Then he threw it back into Vargas's lap. Pastor Rizzo, who must have seen the angry glint in Ryan's eye, quickly followed and tried to wrap his arms around his daughter's boyfriend before he could start throwing punches.

Vargas straightened. His casual demeanor instantly disappeared, in its place a look of contempt. He got up slowly, glaring at Ryan, and for the first time his intent appeared to match his physical appearance.

"Let it go," Rizzo said.

"Easy for you to say," Ryan shot back while glaring down at Vargas. "Why do you think he's really here?"

"The same reason you're here," Rizzo replied in a soothing voice.

But it was going to take more than the pastor's calming influence to de-escalate the situation. Ryan snarled as he struggled to free himself from Rizzo's grip, though not too hard. His relationship with Emma was probably what stopped him from using greater force.

"Why are you here, Vargas?" Ryan demanded.

"Please, not on this trip," Rizzo said. "I know you two have your issues, but think about Emma, Megan, Jim, Maryann, and little Connor."

Ryan let out a dismissive grunt. "This dirtbag took me for two grand."

"Settle that between yourselves, *another time*."

"That's not why he's here," Ryan spat. "He came to cause trouble between Emma and me. Didn't you, Ricky?"

Vargas shook his head. "I'm here for the same reason as you. The great outdoors."

"Since when did you like camping?"

"Always loved it. Didn't realize you were a fan too."

"If the pastor wasn't here, you'd be picking up your teeth with a broken arm."

Vargas leaned over the seat toward him. "You're welcome to try, but I'd advise you cool your jets, buddy. Stop ruining the ride to West Virginia."

Ryan's face darkened. Megan guessed that no response from Vargas would ever appease him, and the situation was rapidly deteriorating. Both men stood within inches of being able to land a punch.

"Ryan, calm down and get back here!" Emma shouted.

"Listen to my daughter," Rizzo added.

Ignoring their pleas, Ryan stepped closer to Vargas.

Megan jumped up from her seat and stood in the aisle, blocking the path between the two men. She surprised herself with the move. Perhaps it was natural instinct, part of her old self returning. Or maybe it was self-preservation.

A dustup between these two would almost certainly spill out into the rest of the bus, perhaps causing injuries to old and young.

"Cool it, now! I know you two have history," Megan said, peering into Ryan's scowling eyes. Beyond him, everyone in the bus except DeLuca had turned in their seats. "I know this might be tough, but for the sake of the trip, for everyone else here, just drop it for three days."

"He's here trying to fuck with me," Ryan replied, still glaring at Vargas. "Causing trouble where he's not wanted."

Vargas laughed. "Do you seriously think I'd get up at five a.m. with a hangover just to piss you off? Get over yourself, bro."

Ryan stepped closer.

Megan gently pressed her hand against his chest, halting his advance. The adrenaline surging through her body made her shudder. They could go off on each other at any second, with her in the cross fire. She blinked, and in that instant, she was surrounded by roaring flames, the desperate screams of her husband and son rising above the crackle.

Switch on, she told herself.

She focused back to Ryan. He must have seen something in her face because he stepped back, his attention now on her. His scowl softened.

"Sorry. I didn't mean to cause you any trouble," Ryan said. "I mean, we all know what you went through."

Megan glanced at Pastor Rizzo, who looked down at his sandals. The subtext was obvious. So much for confidentiality, though, to be fair, probably half the tristate area knew about the worst part of her history. "I'm fine," she said sternly. "What's not fine is two grown men fighting in front of a kid. So do us all a favor and back off, all right?"

Vargas nodded in agreement. "She's right, Ryan. Back off."

"You're an asshole, Vargas," Ryan replied. "We'll do this when we get back."

"I'm sure we will. It's a date." He winked at Ryan, only further pissing him off.

Emma scrambled down the aisle. Squeezing past her father, she grabbed Ryan by the shoulder. "He's not worth it, baby. Don't sink to his level."

Ryan nodded in agreement, keeping the intense stare, but

eventually he turned away and followed Emma back to their seats.

"Go sit at the front," Rizzo said to Megan. "I'll keep Ricky company back here."

"Sure thing."

Vargas scooped up his jacket and leaned back, seemingly unaffected by the confrontation. He either had a great poker face or genuinely didn't give a shit.

Megan grabbed her daypack and headed to the front of the bus. She appreciated that Rizzo was handling the situation in the best way he could, but even the most naive person in the world could see that this wasn't the end of it. She let out a short, ironic laugh.

This tranquil nature outing had taken less than an hour to turn into an episode from *Days of Our Lives*—her guilty viewing pleasure during the past few months.

Maryann grabbed her arm on the way past. "You did good, girl."

"Thank you."

"I've got your back," Jim said, keeping his voice low. "If they give you any trouble, I'll give 'em a knuckle sandwich."

She smiled down at him. "I'll be okay."

"Trust me. Back in the seventies, I was a bouncer at the Beekman Pub. They nicknamed me Gentleman Jim. You see, there used to be a boxer named—"

Maryann elbowed him. "She doesn't want to hear your stories, Jim."

He gave her a reproachful look, then eyed his sudoku-puzzle book.

Megan continued forward, thankful for the friendly support. She dropped her pack on the passenger seat beside DeLuca. He kept their speed at a steady sixty miles per hour.

By her reckoning, they still had at least three hours until the next stop. She unlocked her phone and sifted through the steadily decreasing cache of work emails. The more time she spent away on the self-prescribed break, the more she lost touch with current developments at Hunts Point—maybe to the point of becoming irrelevant.

This sabbatical had to end, whether she liked it or not.

DeLuca looked over to her and said, "You stood up to those guys well. Showed some guts. I was just about to pull over and intervene."

"Pastor Rizzo sorted it out."

"You'll forget all about it once you see Davies Canyon."

"Have you ever been there?"

He shook his head. "Nope. And I bet few people have in the last couple of centuries. It's not easy to get to, but it's a dream location."

"How did you find out about it, then?"

"Google Maps. I scanned the forest for a week, trying to identify something special, something untouched. It's a clearing at the foot of a mountain, surrounded by dense woodland and a river. *Idyllic*, some would say. Pristine. Do you know how rare that is in this country anymore? I am so excited."

Megan nodded. "Me too."

She desperately needed this trip. And despite the bad blood between two of the travelers, this was paradise compared to the horrors of her last outing.

"So once we get there, how far is the hike from the road to the campsite?"

"Oh, maybe two hours max," DeLuca replied. "We should make it before sundown, don't you worry. And if this trip works out how I expect, it'll be an experience that stays with you for the rest of your life."

The final few hours of the trip had been pure torture for Ricky Vargas. The booze-induced headache had subsided, only to be replaced by Pastor Rizzo's constant yammering in his ear. An endless stream of anecdotes about reforming, about coming back to the church, about Ricky's shitty life choices. Some of the questions were highly personal; most were irrelevant.

The man must have Duracell batteries in his larynx. He also loved the sound of his own voice and wouldn't stop talking. Ever. It was like a bad infomercial on a constant loop. His latest sermon, which Vargas was trying to block from his mind, involved an old wives' tale that he supposed was about forgiveness.

Rizzo wasn't a man of God. The devil had sent him to torture Vargas.

Finally, DeLuca turned the bus off the highway and onto a single road. Within minutes, all signs of civilization beyond the road's shoulder had vanished, replaced by lush, thick forest on either side. The afternoon sunshine punched through the canopy here and there, dappling the forest floor with light.

Vargas thought it somewhat beautiful—at least, to people who liked this sort of shit.

Mountains jutted against the distant skyline. Getting out of here on foot wasn't an option. That was cool. He had no interest in playing the role of mountain man—just as long as he could keep track of the group's whereabouts in relation to the vehicle after they had departed for the campsite.

Nothing else really mattered. Not Ryan, who he would never see again. The same applied to Rizzo and his well-intentioned twaddle, and everyone else here. It would be goodbye to these losers forever.

"Not far now, guys," DeLuca chirped through the crackling speaker. "Prepare to stretch your legs on the way to Davies Canyon and to breathe in some of that pure West Virginian air."

Vargas would trade all that pure West Virginian air for a cigarette right about now.

A few miles down the road, the bus slowed past a dirt track. DeLuca began to turn in, then abruptly stopped and looked at his maps.

To Vargas, it looked as if the guy had printed directions off MapQuest.

DeLuca backed the bus up onto the main road and continued driving ahead.

"Whoops," he said to no one in particular.

This happened a few more times over the next half hour. Vargas frowned as he stared toward the front of the bus. Regardless of what he thought of these people, which wasn't a great deal, it appeared that the guide, driver, or whatever DeLuca fancied himself, was about as useful as a one-legged man in an ass-kicking contest.

Rizzo patted Vargas on the shoulder. "Don't look so concerned, Ricky. We'll be there soon enough."

"Not concerned. Just wondering if this guy's gonna steer us into a ditch."

"No, no. Paul has years of experience."

"In what? Are you sure this guy isn't one of the Impractical Jokers? 'Cause it seems like he's screwing with us."

"Have faith, Ricky. If what Paul says is true, you'll want to come back here again and again."

Highly doubtful. "Sure," Ricky said. "I hope so. It seems super easy to get there too," he added, unable to resist the sarcasm.

The bus slowed to a halt by a weedy, rutted track through the trees. Moments later, DeLuca turned in and headed into the darkness of the forest.

"Yo, DeLuca, are you sure you got the turn right this time?" Vargas yelled out.

"Most definitely," DeLuca replied. "This is it. I think."

"Five times a charm, right?"

Vargas rocked in his seat as the bus's tires bumped through depressions in the makeshift road. Bile rose in his throat. Those drinks at last night's card game had come back to haunt him. He should have kept drinking today. That would have stopped the hangover cold.

The bus powered through thick foliage. It appeared that no one had driven this road in a long time—at least, no one with any sense. This really was the wilderness. Was this even a road they were on?

After a few more stomach-churning minutes of bumping and lurching, the bus entered a small clearing. *Parking lot* would have been too generous a term. No trails led off into the dense growth of trees. In fact, the only thing that betrayed a previous human presence, besides the track leading here, was the crumpled, moldy remains of a tent.

"Okay, everyone, it's a two-hour hike from here," DeLuca said. "Grab your stuff, and we'll head straight off. Got to use the natural light while we still have it, so we can build our campsite before dark."

Rizzo quickly moved to the front of the bus, got off, and stood below Vargas's window, no doubt ready to hand out the backpacks along with the appropriate blessing.

Vargas wondered whether a man existed who could be this altruistic, this pure. Surely the old dude had a few skeletons hiding in his closet. Emma had never let on during their time together. It would be fun to find out before he hatched his plan.

The old couple took their grandson outside. He raced around the bus, searching the ground for whatever it was that kids searched for. They grabbed their gear.

Ryan and Emma got their packs next. He eyed Vargas through the window.

Vargas needed to keep Ryan at arm's length—didn't need him screwing the plan up. He resisted the urge to raise his middle finger.

Ignore him. He's irrelevant.

Then Emma glanced up.

Her bright hazel eyes still made his heart skip a beat. In another world, they would still be together. In the end, back when they were dating, Vargas had known he would end up dragging a good person down. So when she dumped him, he did the honorable thing and let her move on. Unfortunately, she took the wrong path and ended up with Ryan.

I may be an asshole, but at least I'm not a douchebag like him.

He sighed to himself as he headed out. Once in the fresh, humid air, he flipped open his pack of Marlboros and wedged one between his lips.

They made me come out here. The least they can do is hang on while I have my nicotine hit.

"This must be your bag?" Rizzo called over.

"Leave my stuff," Vargas replied. "I'll grab what I need in a minute."

The rest of the group had crowded around the rear of the bus, where DeLuca was haranguing them about tree species or some related shit. Vargas didn't care. The smoke filling his lungs gave him all the serenity he needed—that and Pastor Rizzo leaving his damn bag alone.

Every few seconds somebody gave him a look, mostly of contempt or impatience. He knew he couldn't get away without attracting attention on this trip. Too much, though, was a bad thing. After smoking the cigarette halfway down, he dropped it and ground it under his boot.

Then, when everyone had moved to the other side of the bus for another natural history lecture, he casually walked over to his bag. He crouched, unlocked the zipper, and opened it.

The cheap tent and the plastic shopping bag of food sat at the top. He fished them out before wrapping a sweater around the rest of the contents—contents that only he knew about.

Vargas closed the bag and slid it back inside the compartment, confident that no one would break into the bus until he returned. The ass end of nowhere in a national forest wasn't a popular hunting ground for thieves.

"You ready, Ricky?" Rizzo said behind him.

Vargas turned to face him. "Do you usually sneak up on people?"

"Relax." Rizzo peered down at the tent and plastic bag. "Is that all you're taking? No sleeping bag? Stove?"

The pastor had startled him.

Play it cool. As if everything were going to Rizzo's plan.

"Don't need no sleeping bag. Besides, it's, like, ninety degrees out. And if I run out of noodles, I'll live off the land. You know?"

"There's space in my pack. Want me to carry your food?"

"That's okay, Pastor."

Vargas tucked the tent underneath his right arm and carried the plastic bag in his left. Yes, he knew he didn't look the part. But trying to pull it off with the Gore-Tex clothing and the bewildering array of equipment would probably make him look even more suspicious. Better to play the inexperienced but enthusiastic rookie.

They walked over to the rest of the group. Vargas stayed on the periphery, planning to lurk at the back, avoiding Ryan and the general small talk. He wasn't experienced mixing in these circles. Back when he was dating Emma, it became quickly obvious that he had an innate ability to piss off Bible-thumpers.

DeLuca studied a map that was protected by a plastic laminate. He placed a compass against it and pursed his lips. A few seconds later, he pointed into the woods. "This way, people. If you have any questions about the flora or fauna, please ask. I'll do my best to answer your questions on the way to our own little slice of paradise."

"You sure you know where we're going?" Jim asked, passing it off as a joke.

"You'll find out in two hours. Now, please follow me in single file and please keep close. We're heading into uncharted territory. Crossing new frontiers. Our only means of communication is my trusty sat phone."

Vargas looked at his cell phone. No damn signal, naturally.

Everyone murmured their agreement, hoisted their packs, and trudged after DeLuca. Maryann, then young Connor, then Jim. Emma encouraged Ryan to go next, and he flashed Vargas his perpetual sulky glare. Finally, Megan, who seemed the most likely candidate if he got bored enough to fancy any conversation.

Rizzo gestured ahead of them. "After you, Ricky."

Vargas followed Megan into the gloomy forest. Right away, sweat beaded on his forehead. The prospect of a long walk got on his nerves. It would soon get to his lungs. But as long as he could remember the way back, it didn't matter.

Only then could he make his move.

CHAPTER

SEVEN

The invigorating scent of evergreens and leaf litter filled Megan's nostrils. Overhead, leaves rustled in the gentle breeze. Being outdoors had always given her a sense of liberation. The whole place felt alive, uncomplicated. Oblivious to any artificial rules of civilization. Like the distant sound of running water, or the birdsong going on all around her, nothing was choreographed. Nothing had an agenda. It just was.

She tightened the pack straps around her shoulders and adjusted the hip belt, ready for their two-hour hike to the campsite.

DeLuca led the way at an easy pace, maybe because of the older couple and their young grandson. Megan had stayed fit using the cardio machines in her garage and exercising in front of the TV to Shaun T's workouts. Ever since the accident, the whispers and prying eyes at the gym had proved too much. But her in-house regimen gave her confidence.

Her boots sank into the damp, mossy duff. She scanned between the trees for any old footprints, bits of garbage—anything to betray a human presence.

Nothing. This forest was effectively untouched by human hands. Pristine. Exactly as DeLuca had described it. She wondered whether this group were the first people to come this way in decades. No, centuries.

They weaved between densely growing hickory trees, then stopped by a small brook with perfectly clear water flowing over its rocky bed. The brook flowed from the base of a lovely waterfall.

DeLuca crouched and pointed at the shallow bank. "See there, guys?"

He edged forward, pointing his finger downward.

It took Megan a few seconds to see the small olive-colored salamander. It sat just above the small stream, staring at them.

"Here's an interesting fact," DeLuca continued. "Did you know some salamanders are poisonous, and some even have teeth?"

"What about this one?" Emma asked.

He shrugged. "Dunno."

DeLuca picked up a stick and waved it toward the salamander. *Hardly the actions of someone at one with nature*, Megan thought. Then something else caught her eye. Beyond the brook, baby blue against the natural mix of browns and greens, maybe a hundred yards away.

She stepped over the stream, curious about the strange color in the forest.

Emma elbowed Ryan, and they followed.

As Megan bushwhacked through a stand of birch, the view became clearer. An abandoned car with a faded body. Bushes had grown around the sides, and a sapling grew out of the mold-spattered, off-white roof. How it got here without any obvious route in struck her as odd. It had to be a quarter mile away from the gravel path they had driven the bus down.

Ryan swept a branch away from the front grille. "I'd recognize one of these babies anywhere. You see the big chrome chevron and the bumper bullets?"

The two women glanced at each other. The vacant look on Emma's face told Megan that they shared an equal disinterest in cars. The way she saw it, vehicles had always been purely functional—a tool for getting from A to B, reliability being the key factor.

"It's a goddamn Chevy Bel Air," Ryan breathed. "Look at those tailfins! That's V-8 gold-level trim right there. She must've been a beauty in her day."

Megan peered through the filthy windows. The car's day was long gone. In fact, the blackened dashboard and seats, and the scorch marks around the hood, made it look as though an engine fire had ended the Bel Air's career.

Roaring flames jumped to the front of her mind. Screams.

Stop, Megan. Don't think about it.

"How the hell did it get here, all the way in the middle of the forest?" Emma asked. "We're a ways from the road."

"Maybe those missing hikers from long ago," Vargas said. He had loomed up behind them, along with DeLuca. He grabbed the passenger-side wing mirror, and it snapped off in his hand. "Oops."

"Idiot," Ryan snapped.

"What?" Vargas replied. "This thing's a write-off by now."

"No, dumbass. This is a '57 Chevy Bel Air. It's a classic. Treat it with a little more respect."

The men stared at each other for a lingering moment. Emma moved between them. "It still doesn't explain how it got here."

"Maybe the track from the road used to lead right here," DeLuca said. "Those birch trees look pretty young to me. Nature just . . . took over. Mystery solved, people."

Megan frowned. "Are you sure?"

"As sure as dawn follows day."

"You mean 'day follows night'?"

Cheeks flushed, DeLuca looked down at his map. He mumbled to himself before nodding at the woods to their left.

"Let's keep moving, guys. I'd like to be boiling coffee before the dusk draws in."

"Lead the way, Paul," Jim replied.

Young Connor shadowed DeLuca as he set off again. The kid loved being right behind the guide, waving around a stick he had found along the way. The grandparents followed, keeping close.

Ryan, who couldn't take his eyes off the Chevy, snapped a few pictures on his phone. He thumbed the screen, then cursed.

"What's up?" Emma asked.

"Wanted to send photos back to the guys at the garage. But there's no damned signal out here."

"You thought there would be?" Emma replied. "Let it go, babe. We didn't come here to stay in touch with our friends back home."

Ryan continued to circle the area holding his cell phone up, vainly looking for a signal. "Yeah, but the boys will love this. If I can just find a . . ."

"Ryan," she replied, a stern edge to her voice. "Let it go. We're out here to be together. You can look at the car on our way back."

He let out a deep sigh and slipped his phone back in his pocket.

The couple headed off, leaving Megan with Vargas and Rizzo. The pastor leaned against the smooth bark of a beech tree. He mopped his brow with a handkerchief and hoisted his pack.

"You okay carrying that backpack, Pastor?" Vargas asked.

"Don't worry about me, Ricky. It's just my age catching up with me."

"All right, then. But holler if you need a hand."

The two men headed after the rest of the group.

Megan followed last, observing Pastor Rizzo's movements. His excuse about his age didn't wash with her. Yes, he was older than most of the group, though at least fifteen years younger than Jim and Maryann, and they had no problem with the glacial pace set by DeLuca.

She wondered whether he was sick but had avoided mentioning it because he didn't want to be a burden. That wouldn't have surprised her, knowing Rizzo as she did. In the dictionary, his picture would accompany the definition of the word *selfless*.

Regardless, she decided to keep a close eye on him. They didn't need the head of the group keeling over this far from medical assistance.

For the next hour, they moved deeper into the forest. She reckoned they were at least three miles from the bus. The sun had started to dip in the clear blue sky, throwing beautiful long shadows across the forest floor. The temperature had dropped a few degrees, but she was still drenched in sweat.

The sound of running water at the start of the trek had grown steadily louder over the past hour. What earlier sounded like a babbling creek had grown to the torrential roar of a raging river.

In the distance, the sun shone down into a clearing. Beyond the grassy lea, a granite crag rose into the air.

DeLuca stopped and turned to face everyone. "Prepare to see the best spot in the Monongahela National Forest. Davies Canyon, in all her secluded glory."

Connor raced past the smiling guide, bounding through the waist-high undergrowth toward the campsite. His grandparents tried to give chase but were no match for the speed and exuberance of youth. He crowed with joy when he reached the tree line, and his voice echoed off the side of the mountain.

Megan quickened her stride, moving alongside Vargas. For the first time since she could remember, she felt a glimmer of excitement at the prospect of seeing this place of unspoiled natural beauty.

"Surprised he got us here?" Vargas asked her.

"A bit," she said, smiling.

"A lot, I'd say. But whatever. Looks like the dude has come up trumps."

Part of her had seriously started to doubt DeLuca because of his apparently scatterbrained approach. She admitted to herself that she was a harsh judge when it came to organization. She had to be that way when running operations at Hunts Point. But guiding backpackers through dense forest required a different set of skills altogether.

Megan walked to the edge of the clearing—and stopped dead in her tracks.

A steep mountain wrapped around the back of the clearing, its sheer face reaching hundreds of feet into the sky. The green grass was long and lush. Beyond the meadow, white water blasted through a rocky flume it had carved at the foot of the mountain. Loud, foaming, at once awesome and terrifying.

Perhaps it explained why this part of Davies Canyon remained such an unknown gem. No trails led here, and reaching it by water was impossible. Its natural barriers made it a perfect secluded getaway from the stresses of city life.

Unless someone decided to ruin it.

"What do you think?" she asked Vargas.

"It's dope."

"Just *dope*?"

"I'll leave the inspirational shit to Rizzo. This place'll do me just fine."

He flicked open his Zippo and lit up, overpowering the fragrant smell of the forest with the acrid whiff of cigarette smoke.

They crossed the grassy meadow, joining the rest of the group to look around in awe at the stunning scenery.

Nothing could ruin this. Not even Ryan and Vargas's squabbling.

This was Eden. Paradise on Earth.

"I take it you all approve?" DeLuca asked, beaming.

Megan grinned. "It's perfect."

CHAPTER
EIGHT

While the others started setting up camp in the middle of the clearing, Vargas found a secluded spot at the edge of the tree line and dumped his tent and plastic bag onto the ground. He didn't want to be part of any conversation right now. The stunning scenery would keep everyone happy and distracted until they found out what was really going on. By then, he'd be long gone.

He wiped sweat from his brow as he stared back through the forest. The walk had sapped his energy. Probably a bit farther than he would have preferred—he was hoping for a quick getaway.

Don't matter, though.

He checked his watch. Almost six—plenty of daylight left. The backup plan was to wait until the dead of night when everyone was asleep. Luckily, it wouldn't come to that. These were good people—Ryan aside—and he had no wish to hurt them unless absolutely necessary.

Just follow the river back to the bus. This would be even easier than he thought.

He had memorized landmarks along the way. The waterfall. A giant boulder. A fork where a small freshet joined the stream. A hanging valley. All in case he had to use his very rudimentary outdoor skills to find his way back to the road.

If DeLuca can find this place, I can sure as shit find my way back to the bus.

Vargas shook the brand-new tent out of the bag. Poles, a bag of pegs, rain fly, and the orange nylon inner body dropped in a heap. He hadn't pitched a tent since twenty years ago, one lazy summer in the backyard of his orphanage.

Should he go through the motions just for show? It would likely arouse less suspicion.

He wrestled off his leather jacket and dropped it by the rain fly. *But where to start?*

Vargas lit another smoke. Took a deep, relaxing drag. It helped him concentrate on complex tasks. That was what he told himself, anyway. He planned on quitting one day, though it might not be until the day he died.

Footsteps approached behind him.

He tensed, prepared to spin around.

The instinctive response of high alert came from his life on the street—and what was at stake. But then he reminded himself who he was dealing with here.

Vargas stood and turned to find DeLuca and Rizzo. The pastor wore a cream fleece vest that clung to his painfully thin body.

Their supposed guide, DeLuca, had stripped down to a sweat-stained T-shirt, revealing his skinny chest and arms. Vargas could take him easily if need be.

"What's up, gents?" Vargas asked.

DeLuca nodded toward the tent. "Wondered if you needed a hand."

"I'm good, but thanks. May not look it, but I'm a seasoned pro."

Beyond them, the rest of the group had erected their tents in a wide semicircle around a patch of bare dirt. Maybe their place for a campfire. Was that even legal in a national forest? Whatever. It would at least keep them warm while they waited for his return.

"Oh, but there is one thing you can help me with," Vargas said. "It's a little embarrassing, though."

"Oh, try us, Richard," said the pastor. "We're an understanding bunch."

"Yeah, well, it's like this. I pretty much screwed up. Left my meds back on the bus."

"Meds?" Pastor Rizzo asked.

"Yeah, I take insulin."

"Really? Emma never mentioned that before."

"'Cause I never mentioned it to her before. Like I said, it's embarrassing."

"Pish. There's nothing embarrassing about that."

"Back home there is, Pastor. Family history of diabetes doesn't exactly give you much street cred in the Bronx, know what I'm sayin'?"

Rizzo nodded in understanding.

"In that case," DeLuca said, "I'll take you back first thing in the morning. Don't worry."

"No," Vargas snapped back. "I need them tonight."

He drew in a deep breath. *Stay focused.*

Both men eyed him with a hint of suspicion. Or maybe it was his own paranoia creeping in. This was a fairly simple move, yet what rode on it was life changing.

"Are you okay?" Rizzo asked.

Vargas let out a deep sigh. "Look, this isn't something I wanna mess with, Pastor. If I don't have those meds and I go into shock, I'm effed. Better safe than sorry. Look, I'll grab the keys, get the insulin, and be back in time to roast marshmallows. Easy peasy."

DeLuca shook his head. "Can't let you do that, son."

"Huh?"

"The first rule of hiking is never go alone unless absolutely necessary. I'll come back with you."

"Appreciate the offer, but I can make it twice as fast on my own," Vargas replied. "Besides, I don't wanna put anyone out. This is my dumbass mistake; I'll fix it. I know how to get back, don't worry."

"Like any good leader, my first concern is for the group," DeLuca said. "And in your own words, it's better to be safe than sorry. The two of us will go together."

Rizzo nodded in agreement.

Vargas cringed inside. The conversation had started to attract attention. Both Jim and Megan, who had been collecting wood for the fire, looked over from their pile of sticks. The last thing he needed was Ryan to come over with a barrage of questions.

Vargas was a good bluffer, but he wasn't used to bluffing innocent people. He generally stuck with the philosophy of no honor among thieves. Regular folk got dragged into bad situations only when they horned in where they weren't wanted.

"Paul's right. It's not safe to hike on your own, Ricky," Rizzo said. He turned to DeLuca. "Think you can make it there and back before nightfall?"

DeLuca frowned, as if in serious thought, though Vargas doubted that a serious thought had ever gone through the man's mind—at least, not one with life-and-death consequences.

Vargas stood there for an uncomfortable few moments, waiting for the guide's decision. A hint of anger flared inside him. Yes, his insulin story was bullshit, but that wasn't the point.

"We can just about make it," DeLuca said. "But we need to head off right now."

Vargas sighed. "Fine, suits me," he said grudgingly. "We both go."

"Good man." DeLuca turned to Rizzo. "I'll take my sat phone in case of emergency. I'll keep him safe, Pastor, don't worry."

Vargas stifled a laugh.

"Something funny?" DeLuca asked.

"No, not really. I'm just relieved that I'll live to see another day."

Rizzo patted them both on the back. "It's settled then. Just make sure you come straight back. By nine o'clock, you'll be hiking in the dark."

"You got it, Pastor," DeLuca said. He headed to his tent to grab whatever he needed for their journey back to the bus.

Vargas grabbed his jacket. The plan had never involved anyone coming back with him, but he needed those bus keys. And if this was the only way to get them, so be it.

The only thing left to figure out was how to deal with DeLuca once they left the campsite. It wouldn't take much to eliminate him from the equation.

CHAPTER

NINE

Megan zipped up her dome tent to give herself some privacy. Even though the sun was near setting, the interior heated up fast. Still, it got her out of everyone's sight while she spread the contents of her pack out on her sleeping bag.

Her late husband had loved to take the family camping. She had taken some of his gear from the garage. It was partly sentimental but mostly practical. She flicked open each implement on Mike's Swiss Army knife. The memory of taking Ethan fishing flashed through her mind. Cutting the leader. Attaching the sinker. Baiting the hook.

Tears welled in her eyes.

She closed the many blades and put the tool aside, then picked up the small but powerful UV light that Mike had used to spot scorpions when they camped in the Grand Canyon. Not that she expected any scorpions here, but better to have it and not need it.

The same applied for the first-aid kit and water-purification pills.

Next, she unpacked the gas stove and some boil-in-the-bag meals. Megan hadn't felt real hunger for months. The joy had simply gone from food, even from her favorite dish, artichoke française. Nowadays, she ate out of necessity, just to fuel her body.

"Where'd Vargas go?" Ryan said to Emma outside the tent.

The young couple had pitched their tent close to Megan's, near the roaring water. She had chosen this spot because she hated sleeping in near silence. Back home she used a white-noise generator so that a creaking rafter or a tinkle in a pipe wouldn't set her heart racing. She hoped the white water would do the same, masking the snap of a twig or the scurrying of a small animal in the surrounding forest.

"I said, where did Vargas go?" he repeated, the irritation apparent in his voice.

"Back to the bus," Emma replied.

"Huh? Why's that?"

They were keeping their voices low, probably unaware that Megan was within earshot. She kept still, feeling a pang of guilt about eavesdropping, but she wanted to know whether Ryan had calmed down yet.

"What are you looking at me like that for?" Emma asked.

"Back to the bus for what?"

"Dad said he forgot his medication."

"Medication?" Ryan snorted. "You mean he went to go shoot up or something."

"Ricky might be a dick, but he doesn't do drugs."

"Sure, and I can play the saxophone with my ass."

Emma tutted. "The driver, Paul, went with him. I'm telling you, Ricky's no junkie."

"Doesn't matter anyway. The two of them will probably just walk in a big circle looking for the bus. I imagine they'll find their way back sometime next Tuesday."

"Have a little faith. Paul got us here, didn't he?"

"DeLuca got lucky, I'm telling you. Working in a Walmart garden center doesn't exactly qualify you as an expert outdoorsman."

While the couple continued their conversation, Megan took sunscreen and a water bottle from her backpack and stuffed them in her daypack. Her plan for tomorrow was to take a solo walk in the woods. Take in the natural beauty without any disturbances, away from any of the interpersonal drama that she had experienced since boarding the bus.

Ryan eventually left to talk with Rizzo—something about laying down the law so he wouldn't feel the need to strangle Vargas.

Megan unzipped her tent to let in the fresh air. She poked her head out and glanced in either direction.

Emma lay prone on a towel in a polka-dot bikini. She lowered her sunglasses and smiled.

"Thought I'd catch a few rays before the sun disappears. How's it going in there?"

"Just unpacked." Megan crawled out on her hands and knees. She sat down cross-legged, cooled by the gentle breeze. "I've seen you a few times at the church."

"I go to support Dad. Trips like these are my payback."

"So you're not religious?"

"Lapsed. How about you? I mean, you've hardly been around since . . ." She gave an embarrassed smile.

Better get used to these reactions. They'll eventually peter out.

"I'm sorry," Emma said. "I didn't mean to—"

"Listen, you don't have to dance around the subject. I won't ever get over what happened, but it doesn't mean you have to walk on eggshells around me."

"Understood. I hope we can enjoy ourselves this weekend."

"You might have your work cut out for you."

Emma laughed. "Believe me, Ryan's a big pussycat. Always does the right thing—with a little guidance. You can't blame him for being mad at Ricky."

Megan nodded. "Do you trust him?"

"Who, Ryan?"

"No. Ricky."

She sighed long and low. "Ricky is good as long as it suits Ricky."

"That doesn't really answer my question."

"Are you asking me why he came on this trip? If you are, the answer is, I haven't a clue. Ricky has always been hard to read. But don't worry, I'll manage the situation."

"Meaning?"

Emma sat up with a groan and locked eyes with her. "Put it this way: if I keep Ryan under control, there isn't much trouble Ricky can cause out here. I mean, we're in the middle of nowhere, right?"

Megan stared at a couple of clouds drifting through the cobalt sky. She had felt an instant warmth from the confident younger woman. Emma certainly didn't fit any of her preconceived notions of a preacher's daughter. But Megan doubted that her confidence and control would be enough to stave off another conflict between the two men.

* * *

Vargas followed a few steps behind DeLuca, wading through knee-high undergrowth. Thank God the heat of the day had started to wane, but his damp T-shirt still clung to him.

His boots, bought with an eye toward fashion more than utility, squelched on the moist ground. His socks were wet, and it felt like a blister was developing on his right heel. Why DeLuca chose to slog through one of the only damp parts of the forest instead of the mostly bone-dry land, he had no clue. A branch whipped against his cheek. It stung.

And people did this for *fun*? Such minor discomforts didn't matter, though.

As predicted, he had managed to play on the group's naivete. The only one with the balls to call him out was Ryan. Emma, kindhearted, predictable soul that she was, had her boyfriend on a tight leash to avoid confrontation.

Everything was going smoothly.

Unfortunately, good people often never got what they deserved. He consoled himself that they were suffering only minor collateral damage. They were pawns in a much bigger game. Irrelevant in the big picture. And that picture would soon have him sipping cocktails on a beach.

DeLuca veered away from the disturbed ferns that marked their earlier passing. Vargas gave him a few moments to see whether he had been distracted by something just off their path.

For Vargas's own piece of mind, they had to stick with the recognizable route back. But DeLuca kept heading in the wrong direction.

He felt a spark of anger. He wasn't going to let this fool get them lost in the wilderness. Too much was riding on Vargas getting out of here. Failure would ultimately cost him his life. Maybe not today or next week, but someday in the not-too-distant future.

And now his "guide" appeared lost in his own world. Ambling between the trees, compass dangling from his right hand, gazing around as if he had just been dropped on a planet teeming with alien plant life.

This had to stop.

Vargas hurried to his side. "Where are you heading?"

"Back to the bus."

"We didn't come this way."

"It's an alternative route." DeLuca flashed him a smile. "Who knows what we might find?"

"I need my meds, man. Let's explore on the way back."

"We're not going out of our way. I know what I'm doing, Ricky."

"Do you?"

"My day job involves the natural world."

So you're what, an exterminator?

Vargas bit his lip before saying anything else. Little did DeLuca realize, he was sealing his own fate faster than expected. They had made it at least a mile from camp. Nobody would hear a thing. It was time to act.

DeLuca turned and headed back through the trees.

Once again, in the wrong direction.

Vargas followed, now filled with a different sort of intent. Adrenaline pumped through his body, as it always did when a fight looked inevitable. He didn't expect this one to last long. He scanned the ground between them as they walked, looking for something to get the job done with a single blow.

His boot scuffed against a fist-sized rock. That should do the trick. Then he could be on his way without having to go nuclear on DeLuca's ass.

He stooped to pick up the rock.

DeLuca stopped abruptly and turned, eyes wide with excitement.

"I think we've made our first discovery!"

"Yeah? What's that?" Ricky replied, quickly standing upright.

"Look over there." He pointed toward a dark glade surrounded by woods. "You see that cabin?"

The ramshackle building, likely over a century old, had moss covering its sagging roof. Big whoop. It had gotten DeLuca's juices flowing. No doubt he'd already woven it into one of the nutty theories he'd yakked about on the bus.

But what got Vargas's blood pumping was the thought of completing his real job. For that, he needed the keys and to get back on the right track.

"Wanna explore it?" DeLuca asked.

"Dude, are you trying to kill me? What the hell, man? Let's check it out when we return. For now, I need my insulin shot."

"You're right, you're right," his guide said. "My apologies. This is all just so exciting to me. We'll explore it on the way back, then."

DeLuca slipped a notepad out of his jacket pocket and scribbled something—no doubt just blather about his important "find." Then he turned and headed back in their original direction of travel.

Vargas ducked back down and picked up the rock.

From here, he figured the bus was roughly a mile away. Maybe a twenty-minute hike through the forest. The fact that the guide had got himself back on track made no difference. Their chapter together ended here.

Vargas took a deep breath and quickened his stride, closing in quietly from behind. Drawing close, he lifted the rock.

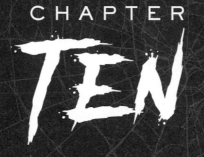

TEN

Before Vargas had a chance to hammer the rock down, bringing an end to his acquaintance with this ridiculous tour guide, DeLuca stepped to the side and crouched by a thick tree trunk. He pointed at a trail of disturbed ferns that snaked down a gentle slope.

DeLuca glanced back to him. "You see that, Ricky?"

Vargas quickly slipped the rock behind his back. DeLuca was temporarily out of range, and he wanted to do this fast and quiet. Yes, they were well out of earshot of the group, but other outdoor freaks might be close enough to hear a protracted fight. He needed an opportunity for a clean surprise blow.

"You see that?" DeLuca repeated, the excitement clear in his voice.

"What?" Vargas replied.

Nothing ahead looked any different. The long shadows of dusk were creeping over the forest, making it slightly darker, but Vargas couldn't detect anything to prompt such an abrupt action. Besides, he wasn't interested in some supposedly rare plant or tree.

"Over there," DeLuca said urgently, jabbing ahead with his finger.

"Over where?"

"Are you blind? Look!"

"At what?"

"You can't miss it."

Vargas searched in front of them again. Previous abrupt warnings like this usually came when a rival was spotted on his turf—a shout to look out or be on his guard. He reminded himself that he was on a camping trip with do-gooders.

He scanned between the trees, trying to locate whatever seemed so important.

A white-tailed deer stood in the distance, staring directly at the two men. It had a majestic rack of antlers. Even though Vargas wasn't a fan of the great outdoors, seeing an animal like this in the wild gave him goose bumps nonetheless.

"Nature at its best," DeLuca whispered. "She's a real beauty too."

"She? Isn't it a male?" Vargas asked. "It's got antlers. That's a dude."

The guide gave him a blank stare. Vargas wasn't entirely sure about the sex of the deer. That said, despite his lack of knowledge about the animal kingdom, he doubted that DeLuca knew any better.

And once again, none of it mattered. The more he delayed, the more he was getting sucked into this man's silly exposition.

DeLuca turned back toward the deer, studying it more carefully.

Now Vargas had his shot. He closed the distance toward DeLuca.

From up in the canopy came an odd high-pitched hissing sound. It was like nothing he had heard since arriving in these woods. Both men instinctively froze. The noise sounded insect-like to Vargas. It reminded him of the creepy sounds he had heard when he helped dump a rival gang member's body in a marsh in the Bronx River watershed.

The thought of the stiff corpse turned his stomach. The pale-white skin with purple blotches where lividity had set in. He was no stone-cold killer. But back then he was younger and had assumed he must get his hands dirty to prove himself.

That corpse was probably a better guide than DeLuca.

Vargas took a step toward him.

No time like the present. Next time he looks away . . .

The hissing grew louder until it reminded Vargas of the white noise from an old-school TV tuned between channels.

Oddly, the supposed outdoorsman appeared equally confused—alarmed, even.

"What's up?" Vargas asked. "You look like you seen a ghost."

"What the heck could be making that racket?"

Vargas shrugged. "Cicadas?"

He shook his head. "Nope. They're more of a ring than a hiss, and anyway, they're not due for another three years."

"Okay, so they came out early. Who gives a shit?"

"They don't—"

A scream cut him off. Short and sharp, like that of a distressed animal. Vargas's head snapped toward the buck in time to see its four hooves shoot up into the canopy. Nothing else moved in the forest.

That was all he saw. Then . . . everything went silent.

DeLuca squinted into the fading light. Sure enough, the deer had vanished.

Almost instantly, the hissing had stopped.

"What the hell?" DeLuca muttered.

He took the words right out of Vargas's mouth. He stood staring, trying to process what he had just witnessed. And now there was only the eerie silence of the forest.

DeLuca moved from behind the tree, peering down the deserted trail. "Now, what kind of creature can do that?"

Vargas stared, nothing to say.

The hissing started again. But louder. The treetops shook and swayed in a path that seemed to be coming toward them.

Vargas stared upward as the thrashing and snapping of small branches drew closer, as if a giant wrecking ball were swinging through the canopy. He covered his ears as the hiss grew louder. It consumed his awareness. Scrambled his thoughts. Disoriented him.

DeLuca stared openmouthed. He gripped the sat phone in his quivering hand.

Vargas instinctively took a step backward.

Branches swayed and groaned above, and leaves fluttered to the ground. The overhead movement crashed on by, twenty yards to their left.

Vargas's heart pounded against his chest as he tracked the movement. He looked back in the direction of the camp, trying to think of a clear way forward.

Then everything fell silent again.

What the hell was happening?

Whatever it is, maybe it's time to run.

Behind him, DeLuca grunted sharply.

Something pattered against Vargas's back.

What the . . . ?

He whipped around toward the tour guide . . .

But DeLuca was not there. The only evidence of his existence was the sat phone—still switched on, but now with a cracked screen—lying where he had stood just moments ago.

The coward freaking ran.

"Yo, DeLuca!" Vargas called out. "Come out, you chickenshit."

He didn't respond.

Vargas glanced around at all the nearby trees. Nothing. His eyes went slowly up into the canopy. A drop of liquid hit his left eye.

"Jesus Christ."

He looked back down to avoid the oncoming rain. But it wasn't raining.

He wiped his eye and wondered at the crimson stain that appeared on his forearm.

Blood?

Vargas drew in a shuddering breath. Being out here in normal conditions unnerved him enough. But this situation had plunged him deeper into the unknown. He swept his jacket off.

Crimson drips fell from the black leather, pattering the already damp ground.

"What the fuck!" he shouted to no one.

The back of his jacket was covered with *blood*. He staggered backward and flung it into the undergrowth.

Vargas spun in all directions, searching for any sign of movement. Any sign of his guide.

"DeLuca!" he bellowed. "Quit screwing around!"

It was more desperation than hope. Someone or something had attacked. His mind raced with what it could possibly be, and how to defend himself.

An eagle? No, of course not—way too small. A bear? Were bears even in these woods?

He had no clue. The sweat beading on his brow trickled down his face. Facing a person was easy. They were predictable. But a wild animal?

It was time to run. But not in the same direction DeLuca went.

Don't need no evidence pointing toward me. Get to the bus; get the fuck outta here.

He took a step toward the trail that led to the road, but stopped midstride.

The high-pitched hissing started again. Scarily close. Honing in on Vargas from the direction of the bus.

The canopy thrashed only thirty yards ahead.

His limited options had narrowed to one. The bus would have to wait. He needed to reach safety fast. That safety lay in numbers, away from where the deer and DeLuca had vanished.

Vargas took off at a sprint, heading back toward camp, racing as fast as he could.

He gulped in air as he bounded through the ferns. Every few strides, he peeked over his shoulder. The overhead thrashing appeared to track him. Always a few seconds behind, but relentless in its pursuit.

He was being hunted.

Goddamn it, I'm not going like this—not with all that's at stake.

His right boot crashed against a rock, and he flew face-first into the undergrowth. Vargas came to an abrupt stop, inches from a boulder.

The hissing seemed to be right on him.

He tensed for a moment.

Get up! Get your ass moving.

Vargas scrambled to his feet and pounded ahead. He had maybe a mile to go.

His lungs burned, though smoking had dropped a notch in his pecking order of current health issues. His only chance was to keep going and hope that someone in camp knew what the hell they were facing.

And that one of them had brought a better weapon than a goddamn pocketknife.

ELEVEN

Flashlight beams cut across the gloomy clearing. Rizzo, Ryan, Emma, Connor, and his grandparents were sitting around the campfire, but they hadn't lit it yet. The pastor was waiting for the two men to return from the bus before they started toasting marshmallows.

Megan had thought it unrealistic for DeLuca and Vargas to make it back here before nightfall, though she had kept quiet. The group already had enough competing voices without her adding to the confusion.

She sat in front of her tent with her Kindle, using the last remnants of natural light to read the novel she'd brought along—a rather fantastical thriller set in the subways of New

York City. A nice hour-long respite from life. She would join the group later and socialize. For now she just wanted to relax and dive into the tale.

A distant cry broke the silence.

Then another, more desperate-sounding scream. Someone in danger. Too far away to know what they were yelling. Loud enough for her to understand that trouble was coming.

She lowered her book, alarmed.

The group all peered into the trees.

"What the hell?" Ryan said. Guiding Emma behind him with one arm, he stood facing the forest, fists clenched.

Rizzo's flashlight beam speared the darkness.

Megan grabbed her Swiss Army knife and climbed to her feet. She headed over to everyone else.

"Is someone in trouble?" Jim asked.

"Seriously?" Ryan scoffed. "Wherever Vargas goes, someone's in trouble."

Rapid footsteps thudded. A dark figure rushed toward the camp, staggering between the trees. Slowly, he became recognizable.

It was Vargas. She could tell by his rangy physique. He burst into the clearing and slowed to a walk, panting heavily. His dark-brown hair was slick with sweat. He propped his hands on his knees, sucking in deep, wheezing breaths.

"What's going on?" Ryan demanded. "Where the hell's DeLuca?"

Vargas raised a hand while catching his breath.

Jim wrapped an arm around Connor. Maryann stepped behind them. The three wore matching blue fleece jackets. Their movements looked defensive, which Megan could understand, considering Vargas's apparently checkered history, coupled with the absence of their guide.

Emma clutched Ryan's arm in a don't-do-anything-stupid way.

Vargas stared wild-eyed around the group, as if something had put the fear of God into him. He tried to speak but only produced a string of stuttering vocalizations. Nothing like the confident man who had boarded the bus and met Ryan's confrontation head-on.

These observations set off alarm bells in Megan's head. Something clearly wasn't right. He wasn't acting like himself.

Rizzo rested a hand on Vargas's back. "Ricky, slow down, catch your breath. Tell me where Paul is."

"I don't know! I don't know!" Vargas gasped. He gulped in another couple of breaths. "He just . . . disappeared."

"Disappeared?" Ryan said angrily. "What have you done, Ricky?"

"The hissing! It's something in the trees. Did you hear it?"

"Huh?"

"Listen. The hissing . . . the trees."

"What the hell are you talking about?"

"LISTEN!" Ricky yelled.

The group fell silent. All Megan could hear was the roaring rapids left of the clearing, the light breeze rustling the woods, and Vargas's rapid breathing. Either he was a great actor, or the fear in his voice was genuine. She suspected the latter.

"Ricky, I don't hear anything," Rizzo said calmly, though his face betrayed a very different emotion. "I need you to calm down. Now, tell us what happened to Paul."

"He . . . he just vanished." Vargas glanced back at the forest. "Something just took him. And it chased me all the way back here."

"Something? What do you mean?"

"I don't know! Something in the trees. First, it ripped a deer off the ground, and then . . . then he went missing."

"*Something* in the *trees* ripped a deer off the ground?" Ryan asked, growing visibly angrier by the second.

"YES!"

Ryan broke free of Emma's grip and stormed toward Vargas. He stopped only inches from the other man. "What did you do to him, Ricky? Tell me!"

"Nothing! I swear! One minute he was there, then he was gone. We heard this loud hissing, then he disappeared. I don't know. I don't fucking know!"

"You don't know?" Ryan asked sarcastically. "You mean you don't want to tell us! I swear, if you hurt him in any way—"

"I'm telling you, asshole, something is out there and it's coming for *us*."

It was already obvious that the others did not trust Vargas. Turning up with such an outlandish story and no DeLuca wasn't going to improve the situation. Megan stayed quiet, though. She didn't have enough information to form an opinion.

"If I did something to him," Vargas snapped, "why wouldn't I just take the bus keys and split?"

"That's probably why you went in the first place," Ryan shot back.

Vargas sprang forward, thrusting his palms against Ryan's chest. The force sent him staggering back.

Once again, Megan decided to move. She quickly stepped between the two men before they could start throwing punches.

Emma must have been thinking the same. She stood shoulder to shoulder with Megan, giving her boyfriend a sharp look.

Ryan shook his head. "You can't believe a word he's saying. Next, he'll be telling us bigfoot is about to raid our food."

"I'm not lying, not about this," Vargas said.

Rizzo gave him a narrow-eyed stare. "Ricky, you must

understand, it's hard for us to believe that Paul simply vanished. There's nothing in the forest capable of doing what you're describing."

"Bullshit," Vargas replied. "I saw it happen. What we need to do is call for help—now. You have to believe me."

"We've got no cell coverage," Jim said, still standing protectively in front of his family. "With all due respect, Ricky, I *don't* believe you."

Vargas's face twisted into a scowl. "With slightly less respect, I don't give a shit. You'll find out soon enough if I'm right."

"Everyone take a deep breath," Pastor Rizzo pleaded. "Let's say that what he's saying is true—"

"It's fucking true, all right. I ain't going back in those woods anytime soon."

"Let me finish, Richard." Rizzo turned to the group. "If what he's saying is true, our communication with the outside world vanished with DeLuca. He had the sat phone on him. I suggest we wait until first light to send out a search party."

"I say we go right now," Ryan said. "For all we know, DeLuca could be lying in a ditch, bleeding to death."

"But if what he's saying is true . . ."

"You can't be serious," Ryan snapped back. "You're listening to a goddamn criminal."

"You watch your words, Ryan," the pastor shot back. At the scolding, Ryan looked away.

"Wait," Vargas interjected. "DeLuca's sat phone was on the ground. He dropped it. But I'm telling you, it's too dangerous to go back out there."

"Do you remember where it was?" Rizzo asked.

Vargas nodded. "Yeah, I think so."

"Can you lead us there?"

"Even if I wanted to—which I don't—it's impossible to find the exact spot in the dark."

"Okay, so it's settled. We'll head out at first light. In the meantime, let's just hope Paul shows up."

"He *won't* show up," Ryan spat. "Vargas has made sure of that. I suggest everyone watch their back tonight."

The group exchanged glances. It was clear to Megan that nobody believed the story. Rizzo was doing his best to stop things from boiling over, though he didn't sound convinced either.

"So what next?" Maryann asked.

Rizzo gazed at Vargas for a lingering moment. "I want to hear Richard take us through the events again, exactly as they happened. In finer detail. But other than that, we wait until dawn—"

"To hell with this," Ryan interrupted. "I'm heading out to look for DeLuca. The only thing to be afraid of in this forest is standing right there."

"You're not going anywhere, Ryan," Emma replied sternly. "You're staying right here with me. We all stick together until we find out what's going on, understood?"

The night had set in, plunging the surrounding woods into darkness. Megan had no real clue what to make of Vargas's story. She didn't buy it entirely, but one thing struck her while she listened to his tale.

His fear was real.

CHAPTER
TWELVE

Vargas stormed away from the group, toward the riverbank. The simmering anger building inside was about to erupt and that would only make an already dire situation much worse. He knew that when he lost it, no one benefited.

Passing between two tents, he resisted the temptation to smash one of them, mostly because he wasn't sure which one belonged to Ryan and Emma, and which to Megan.

"Get back here, Ricky!" Ryan bellowed.

Ignoring Ryan, he sat down on the smooth surface of a log. He could feel their suspicious eyes on him, but he kept his focus on the dark tree line. The fools around the campfire didn't believe a word of his story. They could shout at him all they wanted, but it wouldn't change a thing.

Whatever. I know what I saw. And what I didn't see . . .

He grabbed a branch from the log and snapped it off in his trembling hands. It was the best thing in the immediate vicinity to defend himself with if he had to.

The way those trees thrashed, the speed with which everything happened—whatever in the world *had* happened—it all seemed unnatural.

He shook out a smoke and lit up. The first drag felt as if he had inhaled powdered glass. He stifled a cough and took another long pull. Smoother this time, but it failed to calm him. Nothing would right now.

At any moment, something could rush out of the forest and kill them all.

How the hell do I get out of this place?

Vargas glanced to his right. Moonlight shone down onto the raging river. At least two hundred yards wide. Foaming. Water surging around jagged rocks that protruded above the surface. Escaping on a makeshift raft wasn't an option. He doubted that anything but a fish could survive a run down those rapids.

The mountain face that abutted the camp was sheer, with no apparent route up. Maybe an experienced climber could scale it in broad daylight. Not him, and certainly not Rizzo, Grandma, and Gramps.

The woods were the only way out—the woods he dare not go back into. Every direction spelled death. Everyone would realize this soon enough.

He could overhear the group around the campfire discussing ridiculous hypothetical situations. For instance, maybe he mugged DeLuca for his equipment. Next, and more laughable, was that they had fallen out over which direction to take, leading to a brutal fight. None of their theories made any sense, and he had stopped trying to listen.

Vargas had already figured out his best option for survival. Live through the night, and head out with the group in the morning. Safety in numbers. Or, more accurately, he would stay in the middle of the group when they eventually made their break. When the time was right, he could sprint for the bus and make his escape. Then he could do what he really came here for—unless whatever took DeLuca came back for seconds.

* * *

The campfire flames illuminated the faces in a heated debate about the group's next moves. It was mostly Ryan and Jim, with ideas full of bravado yet lacking in logic. Megan had sat a few yards away from everyone else to avoid getting sucked into the wild speculations.

It was fair to say that panic had set in, and for obvious reasons. DeLuca was missing. Night had fallen. Something sinister must have happened in the forest.

Megan looked away from the flames, up at the starry sky. Even now, months after the accident, she still couldn't stand the sight of fire. But she had to fight that particular demon on her own.

Right now a far more pressing situation existed.

"Let's see what happens during the next few hours," Rizzo kept saying, perhaps to convince himself as much as the others.

In the distance, Vargas stared out from his log at the dark tree line. Through all his repeated interrogations, nothing about the events in the forest had changed in the slightest, which Megan found interesting. He didn't appear to be acting. Also, liars often overelaborated or inadvertently changed the details. He had done no such thing, telling the same story since he got back to camp.

And while she was no expert in reading microexpressions on people's faces, she knew a bullshitter when she heard one. He wasn't bullshitting.

But how could a person simply vanish? And what could this hissing be that agitated him?

"Richard," Rizzo called over to Vargas. "Are you positive you two didn't just lose each other along the way?"

"I already told you."

"Tell us again," Ryan insisted.

Vargas shifted uncomfortably on the log. "The dude was right behind me and just vanished."

"Did you call out his name?"

"Of course I did. No response, except for that sound coming from the trees."

Once again, nothing changed in his story, regardless of the question he was asked.

The fact remained, DeLuca was missing. This put Megan on edge. Regardless of the guide's apparent incompetence, he had found his way here without a problem, and it made no sense that he would leave without telling anyone.

Megan got to her feet.

"Where are you going, Megan?" Rizzo asked.

"Let me speak to Ricky," she replied. "He might find it easier with just one of us talking to him."

"Good luck with that," Ryan said. "Try to find out where he buried the body."

"Shut up, babe," Emma snapped. "Ricky is many things, but he wouldn't attack one of us then come back here. I mean, why?"

"I'm telling you, we should pack up right now and head back. Better than waiting here for him to pick another one of us off."

"Hike miles in the dark without a guide? No way. Besides, if we make it to the bus, we don't have the keys."

"I'll get that bus started, with or without keys."

Ryan shook his head while staring at the fire. Nothing would convince him that Vargas was telling the truth. It was clear that none of them believed the story. Not even Pastor Rizzo. They were all going around in circles.

Megan headed over to the riverbank, where Vargas was halfway down another cigarette.

He peered up as she approached, and shuffled along the log to make space.

Megan sat by his side. "How's it going?"

"I'd be a lot better if I hadn't been chased through the forest and then accused of lying about it. Hell, even *you* don't believe me."

"I never said that, did I?" Megan replied, locking eyes with Vargas. "So let's solve this together, Ricky. Is it possible somebody followed you down here?"

Vargas shook his head. "We're a looong way from the Bronx. You seriously think some pimp with a beef would come out to this godforsaken place?"

"Okay, fair enough. Is it possible DeLuca got lost or ran away when you weren't looking?"

Ricky shook his head. "Don't you get it? One second, he was there; next second, gone. *Poof.* Now, how does that happen?"

Megan looked away, trying to come up with other possible explanations.

"Look, I know what you're trying to do," Ricky added. "But I said what I know and exactly what went down." He drew on his cigarette and blew the smoke away from Megan. "Those guys over there would shit themselves if they'd walked the last hour in my shoes. They *should* be shitting themselves right now. Whatever took DeLuca is still out there."

The moon brightened his face enough for Megan to see the truth in his taut features, his stressed eyes.

That look was not easily faked.

She, for one, believed him.

CHAPTER

THIR-
TEEN

The first glimmer of dawn gave shape to the trees at the clearing's edge. Megan stifled a yawn, though she had never really fallen asleep. No one but young Connor had managed to get decent rest. The naivete of youth must have kept the enormity of the situation from the front of his mind, and he'd spent the past few hours in his tent.

The longer DeLuca stayed missing, the more frayed everyone's nerves got. Smoke drifted from the last embers of the campfire. The scent of burnt wood hung in the cool air. Ryan and Emma had their sleeping bags wrapped around themselves, deep in conversation as they brewed coffee on a portable stove.

Closer, Vargas sat slumped against the log, still distraught. He had fallen asleep briefly during the night but soon jolted awake, like a dog spooked by its own tail. Other than that, he had mostly kept silent, giving Megan the distinct impression that he, like her, was a loner. But he came by it naturally, at least, rather than by self-imposed exile from society.

As far as things in common went, she supposed that was about where they began and ended.

Across the clearing, Jim and Maryann were busy packing away their tent. The old couple moved slowly, likely exhausted after getting no sleep. Every few minutes, Jim peered over to the log, maintaining a brave face, and gave Megan a smile of encouragement while Maryann ordered him about.

Pastor Rizzo leaned against his backpack, staring pensively into the forest. It was one of those moments when Megan could almost cut the tension in the air. She could imagine what he was feeling. He had begun this trip with such optimism and hope. Now it was all falling apart. He was a good man and didn't deserve this stress.

The plan the pastor had circulated during the early hours was to leave at first light. Find the sat phone to call for help locating DeLuca, then head for the bus. That time had come, though nobody was moving with any real urgency.

Megan wasn't surprised. A lack of assertiveness had infected the group. And so had a creeping fear of what might lie ahead in the forest. Whether they believed Ricky or not, everyone was spooked.

When it came to management skills, Rizzo scored low. Not that Megan could blame him. This situation had catapulted him far out of his comfort zone. Her former self would have taken charge by now, but since the death of her husband and son, she was content to remain a mostly passive observer.

Right now, Rizzo was the best they had.

Megan hadn't given up hope for the bungling tour guide.

People didn't just vanish. Then again, deer didn't get yanked into the treetops either.

She needed something to take her mind off the coming trek until Rizzo called everyone to move out.

"Can you give me an honest answer?" she said to Vargas.

"Depends on the question."

"Did you come on this trip for pleasure?"

He eyed her for a lingering moment.

"Well?" she asked.

"Well, I certainly didn't come for *this* shit."

With that, Vargas groaned to his feet and dusted himself down. Not saying another word, he walked over to his tent and took it down. Jim and Maryann woke Connor, and soon, everyone had packed their gear.

The group assembled by the cold firepit, exchanging nervous glances.

Beyond the clearing, only birdsong came from the forest.

Megan checked her watch. Almost six a.m.

"Okay, team," Rizzo said with feigned confidence, "Richard will take us to the spot where Paul went missing. We'll find his sat phone and call for a search party. With a bit of luck, we'll find his keys too."

"Never saw those," Vargas said.

"It doesn't matter. If we can't find the phone or keys, we'll continue toward the road anyway and call for help when we get cell coverage. Okay?"

The group murmured its assent.

"I said okay, people." Rizzo clapped his hands, trying to cheer everyone up. "Look sharp."

Ryan kept putting the stink-eye on Vargas. He evidently still didn't believe a word of his story.

At this point, Megan didn't care. The camping trip had twisted upside down and inside out, and she simply wanted to get back to the comfort of home. This "relaxing weekend" had morphed into something worse than she could ever imagine, and it wasn't over yet.

Rizzo heaved his pack over his shoulder. "Follow me, guys." He headed for the tree line at a fast, purposeful walk.

Megan followed, pocketknife in hand, just in case. She glanced over her shoulder to take one last look at the clearing. The secluded Eden, with its mountain backdrop and the rapids, was unutterably beautiful. But she hoped hell wasn't waiting for them once they left this little paradise. She'd already been there and had no intention of going back.

* * *

Ryan waited for Vargas to follow Megan into the forest. He didn't trust the bastard an inch. With DeLuca already gone thanks to this second-rate gangster and Olympic-class bullshitter, he vowed to himself that nobody else was going down. Especially not him or his girlfriend.

Vargas slowed his pace. Ryan did, too, staying behind him. He assumed that he himself was the next target since he posed the biggest physical threat.

Emma walked by his side as he waded through the undergrowth of ferns and skunk cabbage. Jim, Maryann, and Connor left the camp last. The older couple had a hard time stopping the boy from darting here and there off the path. The kid was excited, searching for wildlife and shouting every time he came across a mushroom.

"Isn't he sweet?" Emma said. She clutched Ryan's hand.

"Oh. Yeah, sure," he replied, distracted. That kid was the last thing on his mind.

Ryan continued forward, treading carefully on the damp ground. He watched Vargas like a hawk as they pushed deeper into the forest. Closer to the apparent point where DeLuca went "missing."

Sooner or later, he expected Vargas to make his move.

And when he did, Ryan would be ready.

CHAPTER

FOUR-TEEN

A knee-deep layer of mist hugged the undergrowth. Vargas moved through the ferns, scanning nervously in all directions for the slightest movement. The sun had risen enough to send thin spears of light through the trees, illuminating the sparser parts of the forest, though the air remained cool.

Every snap of a twig or rustle of leaves made Vargas flinch. He had visions of the blood dripping onto his face, of being hunted all the way back to the campsite.

Any minute now, it could happen again.

He told himself to relax. Not look like a chickenshit. Not get too paranoid, even though he had every reason to. He listened intently for the strange hiss that had heralded DeLuca's disappearance. Of course, the sound hadn't returned, making him look like the liar they assumed him to be. He could feel the group's doubts about him growing by the minute.

Perhaps the daylight would protect them. After all, whatever he encountered had happened at nightfall. Still, he wasn't taking any chances.

And then there was the danger of that asshole, Ryan.

Vargas hated having his back to the enemy. Out here, besides the unseen attacker who took DeLuca, the jacked-up mechanic was his biggest foe. The only one in the group capable of inflicting serious damage.

The guy was a hothead, and no doubt he would try something before they made it out of here.

Rizzo stopped and turned. "How far was it from here, Richard?"

"A few minutes. Look to your left for an old shack. It's just after that."

"You'll need to show me."

"'Course I will."

Just because he wasn't like them didn't make him a monster. Yes, he lived in a different world. That was all. And because of that, a lot more was riding on him getting back to the bus. They didn't need to know that, though. At this point, staying alive was a big enough motivation for everyone.

Well, maybe not everyone.

Vargas peered back through the forest. Ryan and Emma followed roughly thirty yards behind. Holding hands. Both keeping their focus on him without being too blatantly obvious.

Neither he nor Ryan deserved Emma. She was too good, too pure, had too much potential for either of them. Vargas had done the honorable thing and left her when he realized that.

Ryan wouldn't. And for that reason alone, he deserved a good ass-kicking. That would come soon enough, but not today, and likely not from Vargas. He quickly looked beyond the couple to avoid attracting even more unwanted attention.

At the back of the group, Connor continued to be a nuisance, ignoring his grandparents' admonishments to stay close. Vargas wondered whether the little boy was like chum in the water, drawing the predator in their direction.

A few paces behind Vargas, Megan followed, expressionless. He slowed his stride, letting her catch up. The sadness he saw in her touched something deep inside, though he couldn't quite put his finger on it.

No big deal, though. If something came in his direction, having someone by his side gave him a fifty-fifty chance of avoiding the first attack. She appeared alert and would know what to do. It would give him a head start.

The group trudged silently toward their first destination. Vargas's boots sank into the damp ground with every step. Once again they followed the stream, right through the marshy part of the forest. Last night's sprint back to the campsite had wiped him out, and he was still feeling it. But adrenaline had gotten him through, as it would if the thing came again.

As they drew closer to the spot in the forest where DeLuca disappeared, butterflies invaded Vargas's stomach. He swallowed hard, told himself to keep his head. Now wasn't the time to flake. His prize at the end of this trip was still in reach.

"Are we close to where it happened?" Megan asked.

"I don't know *what* happened, but yeah, we're close."

"You know the biggest problem?" she said.

"Yeah, DeLuca's missing and everyone thinks I did it."

"Okay, besides that." She smiled. "Let's say what you're saying is real. Both the deer and our tour guide got pulled up into the trees. You're focused on what did it."

"No shit," Vargas replied.

"The real question is, where did it take them? Because there's nothing in these trees, Ricky."

They both looked upward. A gentle breeze swayed the tree-tops, and beams of sunlight blazed through the canopy, making dappled patterns on the forest floor. The pristine woodland seemed to have entirely forgotten any terrifying doings from last night.

Vargas had not thought of that question. She was right, though. The deer was gone. DeLuca's body was gone.

Where did they go?

He quickened his stride to join Rizzo at the front of the group. As he did, he stared up at the canopy. Everything seemed almost boringly normal, as if nothing had happened here.

Rizzo looked to his left. "Is that the shack?"

"Yep." Vargas pointed to a small clearing several yards ahead. "It's just over there. Follow me."

He stepped tentatively toward the point where DeLuca had vanished, half expecting to hear that infernal hissing at any moment.

The trees were dense here. He remembered searching desperately around them for the vanished guide. Then he had tossed his jacket on the ground. After his panicked dash to the camp, with his mind racing, he had forgotten to explain about the leather being covered in blood—and that he had left it behind in the woods.

Vargas held his arm out to stop Rizzo. "Something I forgot to mention—"

"It's there!" Rizzo exclaimed.

The pastor hurried forward a few paces, crouched, and lifted the sat phone from the leaf litter. It still appeared in one piece, albeit with a cracked screen and dark-red specks on one side. At least, this confirmed part of Vargas's story—though only the irrelevant part.

Emma, Ryan, Megan, and Vargas caught up with Pastor Rizzo as he held the phone aloft. Ryan's face told Vargas that the discovery was simply a confirmation of his suspicions.

To hell with him. With all of them. I know what I saw. And what I didn't see.

Rizzo gave Vargas a grim nod. "Okay, so Richard's story seems based in truth."

"Are you kidding me?" Ryan interjected. "All it tells us is that he probably mugged the guy and left him bleeding behind a log somewhere."

Vargas bit his lip as the realization came upon him. Now that the group had found the sat phone, it was only a matter of time before the cops got involved. And since he was the last person to see the tour guide alive . . .

God damn it.

He needed to lose these suckers fast. He had done his duty as a human being getting them here. If it looked suspicious, too bad. He would be long gone by tonight.

"Your logic doesn't track, Ryan," Megan said. The group turned toward her, surprised at the interjection. "If Ricky is guilty of something, why would he lead us back here to find the evidence?"

Ryan mumbled to himself and turned away.

Vargas's resentment softened at this unexpected defense.

"Okay, but there's still no sign of DeLuca or any kind of struggle," Ryan finally said, eyeing Vargas. "So where the hell did he go, Ricky?"

"Ryan, please," Rizzo said. "Let's keep our cool and just call for help."

The pastor pressed a few buttons on the sat phone, and it chirped to life. White LED light radiated from the screen as he thumbed a button on the side.

"Thank God," Emma whispered.

Megan was watching Rizzo's every move. During the short time that Vargas had known her, he had determined that she was the analytical type. Always observing, rarely wasting her words. The type of woman who usually gave guys like him a wide berth.

The breeze picked up through the trees, shaking branches.

Vargas tensed for a moment. No hissing. He needed to get out of this damn forest, pronto.

"It was channel seven for the Forest Service, I believe," Rizzo said, toggling through the numbers. He raised the device and pressed the side button, activating the walkie-talkie feature. "Come in, Forest Service. This is Pastor Dwayne Rizzo. Do you hear me?"

The radio let out a ping, followed by a static squelch.

"Hello, Forest Service, this is Pastor Dwayne Rizzo from New York. Is anyone there?"

The group waited.

"This is the Monongahela Forest Service, hearing you loud and clear. Forest Ranger Steve Wright speaking."

"Thank you, Steve! Um, yes, so I'm Pastor Dwayne Rizzo from Our Lady of Saints in New York City. Eight of us from our church camped out in Davies Canyon last night. But our guide, Paul DeLuca, has gone missing, so we're calling you for help."

"Is the rest of your group okay, Pastor?"

"Yes, we're all fine and have plenty of water and supplies."

Rizzo looked confidently around the group, stern faced—a man finally back in charge, with everything under control.

"Good. Are you still in Davies Canyon?"

"No, we're in the forest about halfway between the canyon and the entrance road where our bus is parked. We're following the river back toward the bus. I think we know our way to the road.

"Okay, I know the area you're in."

"Our main concern is for our friend Paul."

"Yes, I understand. Can you describe him, please?"

"Uh, yes. Early fifties, about six feet tall. He's wearing a red T-shirt. From the Bronx. Works at Walmart. Um, what else can I . . ."

"Okay, got it. That'll do for now, Pastor. We'll dispatch a chopper to sweep the area and send a vehicle to the road to meet your bus. In the meantime, stay in touch and update us when you reach your bus or find Paul."

"That's great. I can't thank you enough." Rizzo lowered the radio, smiling. "Those guys deserve a medal."

A moment later, the look of relief vanished from his face as he looked beyond the group.

Something had spooked the pastor.

Vargas couldn't detect any signs of movement—only deserted forest and the path they had cut through the undergrowth.

"Uh," the pastor stammered. "Where's Jim, Maryann, and Connor?"

CHAPTER

FIFTEEN

Maryann stood on the trail, waiting for Jim to catch Connor. The top of her grandson's head flashed through the undergrowth from tree to tree. Her husband, red-faced and puffing, chased after the giggling boy. He was no longer built for hide-and-seek.

"I told you we shouldn't have come on the trip!" Maryann yelled.

Jim shot her an irritated glance. "My knee is fine."

"It's not your knee I'm worried about. You're too old to go running around in the woods. We've already fallen behind."

"Don't worry, they'll wait for us. Besides, let him have some fun. He barely got a day camping." He reached to grab the youngster, who sprinted another few feet away. "Darn it, little man, get back here."

Jim gave chase again, breaking into a jog but quickly slowing to an ungainly power walk.

We can't fool around for much longer, Maryann thought. *I'm not risking getting lost in the forest the same way as DeLuca.*

Maryann was convinced their guide had simply lost his way in the dark last night. It was the only logical explanation in her mind, despite Vargas's bizarre story. Ricky probably didn't want to admit that the two men had royally screwed up and gotten separated while hiking. He was just covering for his own ego.

DeLuca will be waiting by the bus, tail between his legs. I'd bet on it.

Ending their trip early didn't bother Maryann. She had things to do at home, like organizing a charity garage sale, and she was already missing her two dogs. Also, this trip wasn't good for Jim's health, never mind his assurances that he was "fit as a fifty-year-old."

But what bothered her most in this moment was the growing gap between her little family unit and the rest of the group. Any more of Connor's antics would put them too far behind, maybe even get them lost, unless someone decided to wait for them.

"Connor!" she shouted. "Get back here right now!"

"Listen to Nana," Jim added in his serious voice. "This isn't funny."

Connor slowly made his way back toward the trail of disturbed ferns, head bowed.

Finally.

She breathed a sigh of relief. He was a little terror, but his unbound spirit was infectious. Maryann loved the time with their grandson—even when he acted like an uncontrollable little shit.

Jim followed, limping a bit. He winced every few steps, visibly trying to cover his discomfort. "Okay, we're back on track. Follow me. I'll lead the way!" he grunted as he walked past her.

That was her husband to a T: always putting others first, no matter what. She could tell he was hurting, but hiding it for the family's benefit. He followed broken fern fronds down a gentle hill. Connor next, then Maryann. She stayed close behind her grandson, ready to grab his little backpack if he strayed again.

A gust of wind whipped through the forest, jostling the sunlit gaps in the canopy. On the ground to her left, something glinted in the sun.

Maryann stopped and crouched, her knees cracking.

Reaching down, she picked up what looked like a gold wedding ring.

She wiped off the dirt and looked at the inner surface.

JSM 1976.

How unlucky.

Guaranteed this guy slept on the couch for a few nights when his wife found out he lost his wedding ring in the woods.

She looked up toward Jim and Connor, roughly thirty yards ahead.

A distant hiss rose above the breeze.

Quiet at first, so she had mistaken it for the sound of rustling leaves.

It quickly grew louder, to the point it could no longer be ignored.

Maryann opened her mouth to call out to her husband . . .

* * *

Connor heard a weird gargle from behind him, like someone clearing their throat.

Nana playing games.

He spun in her direction, grinning.

The forest was deserted. Not a single person in sight.

Hide-and-seek!

"I'll find you, Nana!" he called out. "No counting to ten."

Connor raced away from the trail, darting from tree to tree. Above him, the canopy thrashed in the wind, creating a weird hissing noise in the forest. It all added to the excitement now that she was joining in the fun.

He peered around a trunk, back toward the trail.

Grandpa had stopped too. He gave Connor a concerned look, then yelled, "Maryann? Where the hell have you gone?"

Connor knew it was all an act. Like the serious expressions his grandparents wore when they would scold him but not really mean it. He ducked back behind a tree, out of sight, and looked around for a new hiding place.

He waited, catching his breath, anticipating that Grandpa's hand would reach around the tree at any moment to grab him. Or Nana jumping out of the undergrowth and wrapping him in her arms.

Nobody came.

"Maryann, you're the one saying we have to get moving!" Grandpa bellowed. "Now, quit messing ar—"

A strained grunt followed his unfinished sentence.

Connor let out a loud laugh. This was great!

He craned his neck around the tree trunk.

But Grandpa was missing from the trail.

He's coming after me too!

Overhead, the treetops started thrashing. Connor stared upward, half convinced that his grandparents were doing this to scare him out of his hiding place.

Something wet pattered on the ground beside him.

Red and sticky. It spattered over a fern and dripped onto the ground.

Connor frowned. This didn't feel like a game anymore.

"Nana! Grandpa!" he cried. "You're scaring me. I don't wanna play anymore."

There was no response.

With a rising sense of panic, he looked around him in every direction. Nobody peeping from behind a tree or crouching in the undergrowth.

The overhead thrashing became more violent. The loud hissing built until it made his head hurt. Something was very wrong.

He began to sob, planted his quivering hands over his ears, and screamed as loud as he could. The sound reverberated through the forest.

Suddenly, two sharp points pierced both sides of his head and yanked him violently upward into the treetops. Everything went past him in a green blur until his body steadied, suspended high in the air, legs dangling.

The last thing he saw was the limp, bloodied torso of his grandpa, wedged unnaturally between two thick branches in the tree.

Then the world went black.

CHAPTER
SIXTEEN

Ryan stood glued to the spot, heart racing. Everyone else had also frozen at the sound of a child's distant scream. Then it stopped abruptly, and there was only the muted roar of the river and the tranquil sounds of the morning forest.

"What was that?" Pastor Rizzo muttered.

Ryan looked at the faces around him and saw the same mix of fear and confusion.

They still don't get it.

"Isn't it obvious?" Ryan said, taking command. He stooped and picked up a sturdy stick from the undergrowth. Heavy and damp in his hand. Good enough to inflict a damaging blow. "Sounds like Connor found Paul DeLuca."

Emma took a tentative step toward him. "Are you sure? He sounded frightened to death."

"Wouldn't you be if you stumbled onto the battered body of your tour guide?" Ryan replied, darting Ricky a menacing look. "The kid is no doubt scarred for life."

"Everyone, remain calm," Rizzo pleaded. "Help is on the way."

"Fuck that."

Ryan heaved off his pack, then pointed directly at Vargas. "Don't let this prick out of your sight."

With that, he turned and jogged back in the direction they had come. Ryan knew that if he had stayed with the group, they'd still be debating their next move until the rangers showed up. He wanted to search right now and then lead the authorities to the evidence that would send Vargas to a well-earned stretch in prison. He wasn't getting away with anything again on Ryan's watch.

Rapid footsteps followed him through the increasingly warm forest. He glanced over his shoulder. Emma was only a few yards behind, likely shadowing him to make sure he didn't do anything stupid.

This isn't stupid, though. Finding out the truth never is.

Ryan carefully watched the ground as he advanced, powering up the gentle hill, weaving between trees, jumping from rock to rock. He swept through the ferns. Determination built inside him as he closed in on the site where he had last seen the old couple and their grandson.

After a few minutes, he was sucking air. He had to move fast: first, to bring assurance to the family; and second, to get back to the group before Vargas realized the game was up and attacked again.

I'm the only one he can't push over.

"Would you please slow down!" Emma demanded.

"No."

"Ryan!" she wheezed.

He skidded to a stop by a small stream. "Babe, he ain't getting out of this one, no matter your history with him."

Emma rolled her eyes. "Don't be an idiot *all* your life, Ryan. Are you seriously jealous?"

"Jealous? Of that third-rate pimp? Get real."

"You're behaving like a jerk," Emma replied harshly. "You don't even know what we're running into."

Ryan scanned the woodland in the direction of the camp. The shack was on the right, in dim light under a dense canopy. He recognized the spot where he had seen the family last.

But the place was deserted.

"Jim?" he bellowed. "Maryann? Connor?"

No reply.

Ryan listened intently. Nothing moved except the thick undergrowth of bayberry and sumac rustling gently in the breeze.

Emma caught up and rested with her hands propped on her knees. Sweat dripped down her face. In hindsight, he was happy she had come along rather than staying with her father and Megan. He only hoped the rangers would get there before Vargas tried another dangerous move.

"Guys," he shouted. "It's Ryan and Emma. Where are you?"

Again no one replied.

"Anyone?" Ryan shouted. "Connor, where are you?"

"What's that?" Emma wheezed, scanning the ground.

He followed her eyes to a clump of ferns stippled with thick brown flecks. Moving toward them, he realized that he was staring at spattered blood.

I knew it.

Emma staggered backward. "R-Ryan . . ." she stammered. "We'd better go back. Let the right people deal with this."

"Wait . . ."

Ryan examined the ferns. A small area lay flat. He swiped the tall, dense fronds out of the way to see what had flattened them.

A black leather jacket lay bunched on the ground—the same jacket Vargas had worn until he returned to the campsite with his bullshit story.

Ryan felt the hairs on the back of his neck prickle. He grabbed the jacket's collar and raised it into the air. The back was caked with dried blood.

"Is that . . ." Emma gasped.

"I told you, Vargas is guilty as all hell! This proves it."

"We . . . we don't know what it proves, Ryan."

Ryan bit his lip lest he say something he might regret. The anger welled inside him. He still had no clue to Vargas's real motives for coming on this trip, but murdering a good man for no apparent reason? Sure, Ricky Vargas was a dishonest creep. But *this*?

He peered around the undergrowth, searching for Paul DeLuca's body. It must be close by. He dreaded the thought of finding the bloody remains.

But there was nothing beyond a few blood-spattered ferns.

Ryan walked around the immediate area, searching every inch and seething over the lies Vargas had tried to sell last night.

"Keep your cool, Ryan," Emma said. "Don't do anything stupid."

"You mean like murdering DeLuca? I'm far from cool, babe."

"Forest rangers are on their way. We'll figure it all out then."

"And what if Ricky doesn't wait until then to attack your dad? Or Megan? Or *you*?"

Her eyes widened. "Ricky wouldn't do anything like . . ."

Ryan lifted the bloodstained jacket into the air. "You sure about that?"

She turned back in the direction they had come from.

"I'm not waiting for the rangers," Ryan said, tucking the jacket under his arm. "I'm putting a stop to this right now."

With that, he set off back toward the group at a fast jog. Now he had a legitimate reason to beat the living daylights out of Vargas.

As they approached to within shouting distance and he spotted the figures between the trees, Ryan slowed to a walk. Vargas was sitting against a tree trunk, smoking a cigarette. Megan and Rizzo stood close to him, talking about something.

The adrenaline racing through Ryan's body gave him all the energy and strength he needed to take down this asshole. He hefted the stick in his free hand.

He would circle around behind them, sneak up, and smash the back of that thick skull.

He won't see me coming.

Emma caught up with him. She leaned against a tree trunk to catch her breath. He hated that Vargas had put her in a situation like this. And he had put her father in the same situation.

"Ryan, please, don't walk in swinging."

"And what if he has a knife on him? This stops now."

"You're putting everyone at risk doing this," Emma said. "Let's leave the jacket here. We'll go back and play dumb until the cavalry arrives."

"That's not gonna work. He isn't stupid."

In the distance, Ryan saw Vargas tilt his head skyward and puff out a stream of smoke. How could he act so casual?

Ryan gave Emma a stern glance, then headed off at an oblique angle to Rizzo, Megan, and Vargas. He stepped softly and carefully, not wanting to startle a deer or flush up a grouse and give himself away. Every few paces, he glanced over at the group. They seemed oblivious.

When he was sure he had passed them undetected, Ryan turned. Then he dropped to his knees, keeping the stick in his right hand, and crawled through the undergrowth toward his prey.

He ignored the dew drenching his cargo pants, the flick of a wet fern in his face, the sharp stone pressing into his left hand.

Only two things were important right now: revenge and justice. Delivered by him. Swift and brutal.

Vargas would have years to spend in a prison cell regretting the day he crossed Ryan Andrews.

CHAPTER

SEVEN-TEEN

Megan stared into the clear blue sky, listening for the beat of a Forest Service helicopter. It was probably too soon. Wishful thinking on her part, but it was about all she could do right now.

First DeLuca went missing, and now that scream from the forest. What the hell was happening?

The scream had brought her fully alert, despite the lack of sleep. Her best guess was that Connor had rolled his ankle. Ryan would help him back here, saving Jim and Maryann the struggle of carrying him through the woods.

But that didn't answer the DeLuca question.

In her time, she had dealt with hundreds of bluffers from all walks of life. She could spot them from a mile away. Vargas wasn't bluffing. He believed his own words. Whether the unlikely story turned out to be true was another question. For now, she just wanted to get back on the road to New York. With DeLuca driving.

"You watch, Pastor," Vargas said to Rizzo. "They'll come back and blame me for whatever is going on now."

"Don't be so cynical, Richard," Rizzo replied. "You know Emma. She doesn't jump to conclusions."

"Her douche of a boyfriend does."

Rizzo gave him a faint smile. "He is . . . impetuous."

"Precisely what I said," Ricky replied. "A douche. She's too good for him."

"Emma can be the judge of that."

Vargas squinted as he took another drag from his cigarette. The smoke drifted away on the breeze. He stared directly past Megan in the direction of the bus. His pensive look raised a few questions in her mind.

Although Megan believed him, working out his motivation was an impossible conundrum. It was clear to her that he loathed and distrusted the outdoors. It was like an alien planet to him. He had no good reason to be here and had never offered one. And even after his supposed incident last night, and the terrifying scream they just heard, Ricky still seemed suspiciously preoccupied with other things.

Little by little, she could feel her old self clicking back into action as she studied Vargas. Her skill at piecing together complex puzzles, her ability to analyze events and assign probabilities. Everything pointed to his guilt.

And yet . . .

Behind the tree that Vargas leaned against, some tall ferns moved, pulling Megan from her thoughts. She peered into the gloom.

Then, closer, a sapling trembled. Something was coming directly at Vargas.

Rizzo hadn't noticed. He gazed down at the sat phone, waiting for a response.

Whatever it was moved closer still.

Megan squeezed her pocketknife. She shuddered. Human or animal, she expected a fight.

Just as she opened her mouth to shout a warning, Ryan's head rose above the ferns. Crouched only a few paces from the small clearing, he put a finger to his lips, then raised a hefty stick in his right hand. More of a club, actually.

Was he going to attack Vargas? What did he find?

She couldn't ask him outright. It would blow his cover. Then again, she had seen the animosity between the two men, and she refused to stand by and watch the trip descend into violence when the guide was already missing and the Johnson family was nowhere to be seen.

"Ricky," she said. "Can you come here for a minute?"

"What for?"

"I need help with something."

Vargas let out a heavy sigh. He flicked his cigarette to the side, then walked over to her. Behind him, Ryan had bobbed back down into the ferns.

She needed to manage this situation now, before it spiraled any further.

"What does a woman like you need from a guy like me?" Vargas asked.

Megan ignored the question and peered beyond him at the forest. "Hey, Ryan, is that you?"

Vargas and Rizzo both looked between the trees.

Ryan rose to his feet, holding a makeshift club in one hand and a black leather jacket in the other. His cover blown, he glared at Megan as he stepped into the clearing. Then he threw the jacket down by Vargas's boots. "Care to explain that?" he snapped.

Ricky eyed the club in Ryan's hand. "Care to explain *that*?"

"Answer the question, asshole," Ryan shot back, raising the stick menacingly. "Why did we find your leather jacket hidden in the forest, covered in blood?"

Vargas looked at Pastor Rizzo, whose face was now full of fear. "I tried to tell you earlier, Pastor," Vargas said. "I dumped it last night after DeLuca disappeared."

Ryan strode toward him, club in hand. "It's got bloodstains all over it, Ricky! What did you do to him?"

"Man, I didn't do nothing," Vargas replied. "That blood is on the *back* of my jacket. Something sprayed me. I turned, and DeLuca was gone. Like I told you. I threw it away when I was escaping."

"You are so full of shit."

"It's the truth, I'm telling you all!"

Megan could see that Ryan was ready to swing. His chest heaved. He stared at Vargas like a heavyweight contender at weigh-in, his intent clear.

"Out of the way, Megan," Ryan demanded. "He's not doing the same to us."

Rizzo, reliably kindhearted but ineffective, moved to Vargas's side. "You've got to admit, Richard, this doesn't look right."

"It looked even worse yesterday evening."

Emma entered the clearing and stood by her boyfriend's side. "Ricky," she said, "if you've done anything stupid, now is the time to tell us."

"Think about it, Emma. What reason do I have for ghosting DeLuca, returning to camp, then showing you where it all happened?"

"To make yourself look innocent," Ryan said. "You're staying right here until the rangers show up. You so much as move an inch, and I'm taking you down. And you will *not* be getting back up."

Megan didn't sense danger from Vargas, but a hint of desperation crept over his face. His eyes darted between Ryan and the direction of the bus. She thought he was going to run at any moment. Had he fooled her after all?

"He's right, Richard," Rizzo added. "We wait here until the Forest Service arrives to help. But in the meantime, let's put that weapon down, Ryan."

Rizzo walked over to Ryan and reached for the club.

Ryan drew it away from him. "I respect you, Pastor. But the game has changed."

"Okay, I get that. Just stay calm, please. Now, did you find Jim, Maryann, or Connor?"

"No, Dad," Emma replied. "I thought they'd be back here by now."

Vargas grunted. "Suppose you reckon I killed them too."

"I'll bet a million bucks you're responsible for them going missing as well," Ryan shot back.

"Yeah, bro," Vargas replied. "I killed them while hiking through the woods a hundred yards ahead of them." He gave his head a weary shake. "We'll be safe only when we're out of this damned forest."

"We'll be safe when you're behind bars," Ryan growled.

Megan pitied Pastor Rizzo. The sweat beading on his brow seemed a lot for just light exertion in the mild morning air. His sunken eyelids and slumped posture made him look like a sick man. He was clearly not equipped to handle this baffling situation.

It wasn't worth questioning him at this point. They all had enough to deal with, and Rizzo clearly didn't want to discuss his health problems.

The sat phone chirped to life.

All eyes went to the pastor.

"Pastor Dwayne Rizzo's group," a crackly voice said through the speaker. *"This is the Monongahela Forest Service chopper. Are you there?"*

"Hearing you loud and clear," Rizzo replied with undisguised relief.

"We're approaching Davies Canyon. What's your current location?"

"About halfway between the mountain and the road. We're in a small clearing."

"You said you parked your bus at the end of the road?"

"Yep. It's only a couple of miles from the campsite. Close to the river."

"The river?"

"That's what I said. You can't miss us."

"Pastor, the river doesn't pass through the canyon."

Rizzo's smile dropped. "I don't . . . I don't understand."

"We're above the road now. Um, there's no bus here."

"It has to be there," Rizzo insisted. "Unless it's been stolen."

"Do you hear or see the chopper?"

Rizzo looked skyward. Megan lifted her head, already knowing the answer.

The sky was clear. The forest was silent.

"Uh, no. No, we don't," Rizzo stammered.

"Pastor, are you sure *you're in Davies Canyon?"*

CHAPTER

EIGH-
TEEN

The rising sun shone directly in Vargas's face. He shielded his brow, keeping a close eye on Ryan.

This punk could go off like a volcano at any moment.

That wasn't his biggest problem, though. He could easily take the guy. What he couldn't take was the other thing coming his way if he didn't do something.

With the Forest Service closing in by road and air, four people missing, and him as a person of interest, it would bring too much heat.

Vargas toyed with the idea of running. He doubted any of these losers would catch him before he reached the bus. One of his memorized landmarks was only a few hundred yards through the woods, meaning he could get back from here without getting lost.

But then what?

Fleeing would make him look guilty. At least two people here would point the finger at him for a crime he never committed.

Then I'd have to hitch a ride as a wanted man.

Every option in his mind carried big risk. The saving grace was that DeLuca appeared to have led the group to a different part of the forest—*not* Davies Canyon. That meant a delay in locating the group. But for how long? He had no idea, but it gave him some breathing space to think things through.

Rizzo hunched in the center of the clearing, slowly turning while gripping the sat phone. He had the expression of a puppy dog, silently pleading with everyone to stay peaceful until help arrived.

Ryan and Emma were whispering, glancing over at Vargas every few seconds. Those two were damn sure not deciding his fate. If she had her head screwed on right, she'd tell the mechanic that they were finished.

The only one who looked calm was Megan. She stood beside Vargas, staring up in thought. If anyone here could work out what the hell had happened, he supposed it was her. She was the only one smart enough to realize he wasn't lying—at least, not about yesterday evening.

A faint buzz filled the air.

Vargas tensed.

So much for space to think.

"It's the helicopter!" Emma blurted.

"Thank God," Pastor Rizzo said, pressing the transmitter on the sat phone. "Forest Service, we hear you approaching! You must be close!"

"Ten-four. We're on the lookout for you."

Ryan wrapped his arm around Emma. "Not long now, baby."

All eyes looked toward the clear cobalt sky.

Vargas peered up, though an alarm went off in his head.

The thrumming sound grew louder, closer, though nothing appeared overhead.

Rizzo peeled off his jacket and waved it in the air. He walked around the edge of the clearing, ducking in and out of trees. Vargas wondered whether that would make a difference. He hoped not. Any airlift out of here would take him straight in for questioning.

Last chance to make a break for it . . .

Megan edged toward him, interrupting his train of thought. "That doesn't sound like a helicopter to me."

Vargas saw the concern on her face. He focused on the building sound.

Then it hit him.

The breeze, carrying the sound from a greater distance than last night, had distorted the constant rhythm. It was the same eerie cadence from before.

Before he had a chance to react, it closed in fast, confirming his suspicions.

Somewhere to the left of the group, maybe thirty yards away, the canopy shuddered.

Vargas froze. His eyes went to the source of the noise.

In a dark patch of woodland, leaves fell to the ground. Several birds burst into the sky.

"What the fuck," Ryan muttered.

Within a heartbeat, branches thrashed, coming directly at them with alarming speed, as if a fast boat were racing over the top of the forest.

"Get down!" Vargas yelled. "Now!"

Megan dropped beside him.

Ryan and Emma, still close to the center of the clearing, simply stared at the approaching racket. Much like DeLuca and Vargas when they experienced the same phenomenon. No frame of reference existed for what to do, apart from running.

No one had time to think, though.

Rizzo looked at the tree directly above him. His eyes widened and his mouth hung open. He raised a shaking arm protectively over his head.

Something huge and black scuttled down the tree trunk. Smooth and lightning fast. A dull oval shell over a body the size of a large alligator. Eight chunky legs had moved nimbly down the trunk. A chilling, rhythmic movement that seemed unnatural.

But this was a living thing.

Vargas could scarcely believe what he was seeing.

The monster opened its mouth over Rizzo's head, revealing two glinting yellow fangs like those of a saber-toothed cat.

In the blink of an eye, the fangs sank into Rizzo's head, and blood sprayed everywhere.

The pastor's arms flailed for a few seconds, then his body went limp.

Emma screamed. Loud, long, and bloodcurdling.

Vargas staggered backward and tripped. As he fell, he reached up and yanked Megan back, away from the creature. She landed hard beside him on the ground, but that appeared to be the least of her concerns.

The creature, which looked like some sort of huge prehistoric arachnid, scuttled back up the tree and was gone in seconds, easily carrying Pastor Rizzo's body with it.

The last thing Vargas saw were the pastor's sandals disappearing into the canopy, just as the deer's hooves had done yesterday.

Branches thrashed overhead, and the disturbance receded back into the woods as fast as it had arrived.

The hissing grew quieter. Now its source was known—and more terrifying than Vargas had ever imagined.

Moments later, the forest fell silent once again.

Ryan stood in front of Emma, still holding the club, staring in disbelief. She had her hand cupped over her mouth. Tears streamed down her cheeks.

Emma sank to her knees and screamed again, overcome with shock, grief, and desperation at what they all had just witnessed.

Now only four of them remained. And Vargas had a feeling that number would shrink to zero if they stayed here any longer.

"We need to move!" Megan shouted to the group.

"You read my mind," Vargas said. "Let's get the fuck outta here."

Megan scrambled to a standing position. "Ryan, Emma, I can lead us back to the bus. We have to go, NOW!"

Both stared at her for a brief moment, then looked back out into the forest.

The sound was growing louder again, the thrashing closer.

The thing was coming *back*.

And it was coming from the direction of the bus.

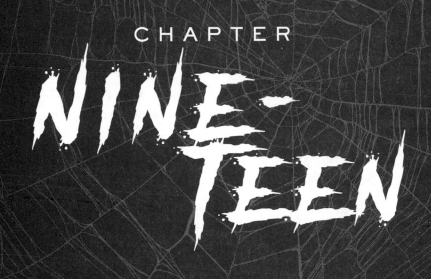

CHAPTER

NINE-TEEN

Megan concentrated hard to accept the reality of the situation and not go into a meltdown. In less than a minute, her reality had been turned upside down once more. History was repeating itself in a different way—the impossible rearing its ugly head to destroy her world again. This time, however, the horrific threat remained firmly in play, and she had little doubt that it was coming for everyone.

Her throat tightened, and her limbs felt stiff and clumsy—much like what she had experienced during the disaster at the state fair.

Images of Ethan and Mike in the burning food stall flashed through her mind. The crackle of splintering wood and burning flesh . . .

The hissing in the forest grew louder, snapping her into the present. It grew so loud that she felt a splitting pain in her temples and ears.

The option of running to the bus had vanished about a second after she shouted the idea. That way was now cut off by the monster.

Vargas, Ryan, and Emma stared at the forest with fear in their eyes. No one moved. No one listened to Megan's command to run.

Ryan, his face now pale as ashes, dumped his pack and fished out a tent pole. He clutched it in a two-handed grip.

No one uttered a word.

She guessed that everyone was in a similar state of shock.

Think, damn it. The bus is cut off. Where do we go now?

They had to do something, and fast if they didn't want to go the same way as DeLuca, Rizzo, and probably the Johnsons. The time for making sense of what they faced would have to come later—if *later* found them still alive . . .

The speed of the thing's approach meant they had no time to lose.

Reaching the bus was out of the question. Megan turned in the opposite direction. They couldn't make it to the campsite clearing without getting attacked. And the river was a nonstarter—they would never survive the rapids.

Think . . .

The cabin.

For all she knew, the giant arachnid could blow through the walls as if they were Styrofoam. But it might provide some cover, and maybe even something to defend themselves with. It beat staying in the open. There was no other choice.

She grabbed Vargas's arm. "Ricky!"

He glanced at her, then back at the thrashing in the trees, now maybe a hundred yards away. The fact that he had been proved right—in a terrifying way that no one could ever have imagined—didn't make the slightest difference.

"The cabin!" she yelled. "It's our only option!"

Emma looked over her shoulder. Her lips trembled as she tried to mumble a response, but she produced only unintelligible stutters.

"We need to move," Megan said. "RIGHT NOW!"

"We won't make it!" Ryan snapped.

The thrashing in the canopy surged past the clearing and made a wide arc coming back, like a shark honing in on its prey.

As the creature rushed through a patch of sunlight, Pastor Rizzo's bloody leg swung briefly into view from the treetops. Limp, with a sandal hanging from the toes. Then it flipped back up into the greenery, thudding against a branch before disappearing from view once again.

Emma gasped. "NO! We have to do something. I mean, he might still be—"

"Emma, listen!" Megan shouted forcefully. "There's no time right now. We go to the cabin. Now, goddamn it. Everybody, RUN!"

Ryan grabbed Emma and forced her to run in the direction of the shelter.

Vargas didn't move. He still stared in the direction of the bus, as if trying to figure out a route.

Surely, he couldn't be thinking about going that way. He might be an idiot, but he was not a suicidal fool.

"Ricky!" Megan yelled. "Snap out of it!"

He shook his head. "Fuck it. All right, let's go!"

Vargas spun away from the thrashing and took off at a sprint.

Megan followed, back into the patchy light of the woods. Ryan and Emma had already covered a lot of ground, following their previous trail through the ferns.

The hissing thrum followed. No matter how fast they hurtled through the woods, it never waned. They could not outrun it.

Vargas took long strides and drew away from Megan.

Behind them, branches groaned and cracked.

Birds squawked and fussed.

Megan glanced back.

Leaves and small branches drifted down from above. The thing had methodically followed their route, all the while carrying Pastor Rizzo's body in its clutches. The thought of his corpse being hauled through the canopy, snagging on branches and deadwood, turned her stomach. She wanted to scream for help, but what would be the point? They were nowhere near where DeLuca had thought, and this time the sat phone was gone.

Megan drew in long breaths and watched the ground ahead. Her headlong sprint had slowed to a fast jog. She feared burning out at this pace and imagined herself slumped against a tree, wheezing. Waiting for the inevitable. Having no energy to put up a last, desperate fight for survival.

Not happening.

Ferns whipped her legs as she ran. Her boots sank into the soft ground. At any moment, she expected the thrashing to move directly overhead, and the monstrous bug to drop down and impale her on its horrid fangs.

Vargas and Megan closed to within several yards of Ryan and Emma. At last, the old ramshackle cabin loomed into view.

The couple's pace had slowed when they got there. Vargas and Megan traced their steps.

The undergrowth was far thicker here. Tangles of blackberry dragged against her boots and scratched her shins. Grunting, Megan powered forward, snapping stalks and stems. Still two hundred yards to the cabin.

From here, the structure looked relatively intact. Thirty feet long with a rusty corrugated roof. The lower part of the log walls was covered in a thick growth of moss. The higher parts were darkened by dampness and the unforgiving passage of time. She saw no visible entrance on this side. Only a dust-covered window with a rotting frame.

The hissing grew to an unbearable volume as the group neared the cabin. Megan resisted the temptation to cover her ears again. She needed her hands to swipe foliage out of the way or to break her fall if she should trip.

Branches hit the ground somewhere close, but she dare not look. One wrong step might finish her. Gritting her teeth, she plowed through the last of the undergrowth, joining Vargas under the cabin's eaves.

"Holy shit," he whispered as he looked back.

Megan planted her hand against the wall, panting. "Is it close?" she breathed.

"It's circling us in the treetops."

She peered around the corner of the cabin. Sure enough, leaves dropped all around, like green snow.

"Found the door!" Ryan yelled from the other side of the structure.

Megan raced around the side of the cabin.

She saw no footprints on the ground. No sign of modern-day visitors.

The roof looked like an old-school Dutch design, hammered

together with large hand-forged nails. The structure looked to be over a century old. Centuries, even, if it had belonged to the original Quaker settlers.

Emma stood behind Ryan. They had stopped in front of a solid wood door.

He slid a dark-red steel bolt along its rail, twisting and shaking it up and down to move it. The screech of metal against metal was like nails on a chalkboard, though it induced less of a shudder than the hissing that continued to home in on them.

Vargas raced to Ryan's side. He slipped off his belt, looped it around the end of the bolt, and heaved as Ryan twisted.

"Hurry!" Emma shouted while glancing at the treetops.

The horror above was closing in on them in tighter and tighter circles.

Megan figured they had mere moments before the monster would descend and snatch its next victim. She glanced at the pocketknife in her hand. It looked pathetic—the equivalent of trying to stop a cannonball with a baseball bat.

The bolt on the door finally let out a hollow snap.

Vargas cocked his leg and kicked. The jamb shuddered, but the door stayed firmly shut.

"Out of the way," Ryan snarled. He turned his side to the cabin and charged. He grunted as his shoulder connected and the door flew open.

Ryan staggered inside and turned. "Get the hell in here!"

Emma dived into the dimness. Then Vargas.

Megan rushed in last and flung the door shut behind her. She breathed in musty air and blinked in the murky light.

The place looked full of dark clutter.

More importantly, the door's inside bolt had a lot less rust. She shot it across, locking it in place. But she had serious doubts that this decaying structure would repel anything with such frightening strength.

She prayed the cabin would hold.

CHAPTER
TWENTY

Vargas shivered at the nightmarish thrum coming from beyond the cabin walls. The creature knew their exact location. He was sure of that. The fact that they were no longer outdoors didn't ease any of his internal terror. They had simply gone from exposed to trapped in a flimsy, decrepit cabin.

The sheer size and strength of the thing . . . How was this *possible*?

Everyone else took a second to catch their breath while standing with their backs against the door. From what he could see in the thin light, the wooden walls were covered in scratches. Maybe someone went insane in here, driven to madness by the deafening hiss outside. Maybe it was the arachnid. Whatever the case, it made this place feel only marginally safer than outside.

Vargas shook as if from an awful hangover. The humid, cloying air made him sweat. He swallowed hard to wet his parched throat.

Now that he had a moment to process the events of the past few hours, his mind raced at warp speed. He tried to blot out the image of the ungodly monster. Never in his wildest nightmares had he conjured such terror in his mind's eye. He pictured the thing scuttling down and grabbing DeLuca, right behind his back. And him standing there, oblivious to the danger while it dragged the useless guide upward.

Vargas didn't want to imagine what had happened next.

He had thought the drug lords and wiseguys in the Bronx were brutal. They were like Bambi compared with the unrelenting brutality of the hissing demon outside.

So what to do now?

It didn't matter that he'd been proved right. Or that he was off the hook as a suspect in DeLuca's disappearance. As far as he was concerned, they all would soon disappear unless an unforeseen twist of fate somehow saved their asses.

"Barricade the windows and door with anything you can find!" Megan ordered.

Her tone surprised him. He'd thought she was a mouse. Granted, a smart mouse, but since the attack on Rizzo, she appeared to have more balls than everyone else put together.

At the far end of the cabin, weak light streamed in through the filthy window, revealing an ornate wooden cabinet and some old-fashioned hoes and adzes propped against the wall. Ryan and Emma moved in that direction. They slid several mold-spattered tea crates out of the way then began walking the cabinet, one side at a time, toward the window.

Vargas flicked open his Zippo lighter and thumbed the flint wheel. The flame illuminated a million dust motes in the thick, musty air around him. He stepped away from Ryan and Emma, toward the darker end of the room. Megan moved by his side, scanning from left to right.

Cobwebs covered everything. Two leather satchels. Different-sized wooden barrels. Decaying tools. Frayed rope. Rags that were once probably someone's clothes. A solid desk and chair at the end.

Various objects cluttered the desk. An inkwell. A brass balance. Other things he didn't recognize but guessed might bring a few dollars in an antique store.

"That'll do for the door," he said, kicking the thick wooden leg.

Vargas moved to one end of the desk, Megan the other. He wrapped his fingers underneath and lifted.

The weight surprised him. Sure, it wasn't as heavy as the particle board from Ikea, but to haul this piece of furniture into the wilderness seemed impractical. Could it have been made out here? Regardless, it would do just fine for a barricade.

He spun the desk toward the door and dragged it across the floor. His right knee buckled, and he silently cursed his unsteady legs. It wasn't the weight of the furniture that had made him sink down. It was the weight of his fear.

"Keep going," Megan encouraged, pushing from the far end.

The legs scraped on the wooden floor planks, making a racket, though not enough to compete with the infernal hissing outside.

It seemed only a matter of time before the abomination crashed through the roof.

Or through the door if we don't get this in place.

Vargas joined Megan at the other end of the desk. They turned it on its side and shoved it firmly against the door.

The natural light from the window vanished shortly afterward as Ryan and Emma moved the cabinet into position.

Next, they moved the tea crates behind the desk and cabinet for added support. Maybe it was pointless, maybe not. There was no way to barricade the damn roof.

Vargas wished he had his Glock to blow that spider motherfucker back to whatever hell world it crawled out from.

He swiped several cobwebs from the corner of the room, revealing a pile of horseshoes. He went to pick them up.

The whole cabin shook, as if it had been jolted by an earthquake.

Vargas swept his lighter from left to right, checking for damage to the walls. All eyes followed the lighter's flame.

Ryan, Emma, and Megan were crouched near the center of the cabin. They all peered up at the shuddering roof.

Dust sifted down from the support beams, showering everyone below.

The heat from the Zippo's metal case grew painful against Vargas's fingers. He flicked it shut.

The cabin shook again.

Cracks of natural light streamed through several gaps in the planks, only to close again when everything went still.

A flashlight blinked on.

Megan angled the thin white beam toward the ceiling.

"Will the roof hold?" Emma cried out.

No one answered. No one took their eyes off the ceiling.

"Ricky," Megan whispered loudly. "Get over here."

"Why?"

"If that damned thing comes in, we'll fight it together."

It made sense in a situation where not much else did. Her clarity of mind had a calming influence. But only in the same way that a shot of rum calmed a soldier from the Great War, clambering out of a trench and charging into a hail of gunfire.

This wasn't quite the calm before the storm. It was the incessant noise before the slaughter. Then again, he had no idea what else they could do.

The group ducked down, backs together, staring around them and waiting for a plank to suddenly crash in, or the roof to collapse.

The hissing slowly grew quieter—still nearby, though not immediately on top of them.

"What do you think it's doing?" Ryan asked. "Leaving?"

"Who knows what the hell it's doing!" Vargas growled. "I doubt it's gonna leave us to casually wander out of the forest."

"You know what I mean, prick."

"Yeah, I do. The situation is that we're stuck here, hiding from a monster straight out of a horror movie. And you asked us if we knew what it was doing—"

"Shut the hell up, both of you!" Megan yelled.

Her voice carried authority. It reminded Vargas of the vindictive bitch of a principal at his high school. Only now, he knew that Megan had spoken for everyone's good.

Ryan shook his head and went to comfort Emma. This, on top of seeing her dad get snatched into the treetops by a giant bug, had pushed her to the brink of a meltdown.

Vargas stopped himself from saying, "everyone be cool," since he wasn't capable of doing that himself. Instead, he moved closer to the wall and listened, trying to gauge when a final, desperate fight to the end was coming.

The arachnid wasn't going anywhere, and he doubted they had the power to withstand the eventual attack.

Should he make a run for it? A lot was still riding on his making it back to the bus.

"Hear anything different?" Megan asked him.

"Nope. Maybe it's just waiting us out."

"I would. We can't stay in here forever."

"But people are looking for us, right?" Emma asked. "The helicopter might scare it away."

"What helicopter?" Vargas asked. "We're in the wrong goddamn woods, 'cause DeLuca took us the wrong way. You heard that ranger. This ain't Davies Canyon. They don't know where the hell we are."

"He's right," Megan said. "We should assume we're on our own for a while. Let's look around in here, see if there's anything useful."

"You serious?" Vargas added. "Shit in here's gotta be from the Civil War."

"Actually, looking at the furniture, I'd say Revolutionary War," Megan said, scanning about her. Her flashlight beam cut past Emma and settled on a gunnysack, covering something lumpy.

Emma reached over and folded back the rough burlap. She cupped her hand against her mouth and gasped, then gave a loud sob. Ryan put his arm around her.

A bare skeleton, shrouded in webs, lay spread on the floorboards. The bones rested on a long wool coat. Hobnail boots covered its feet.

Vargas leaned in for a closer look. As he did, the distant hissing filled his ears, like a nightmare version of tinnitus.

It was impossible to say if the thing outside had ended this person's life. The yellowed bones and antiquated clothing made it look old.

It seemed this pristine forest they'd blundered into hadn't seen visitors for hundreds of years. Or maybe, like the skeleton on the floor, those who entered the forest never left.

One thing was becoming clear for Vargas: if he didn't come up with an escape plan soon, his dream, already on the brink of disaster, would finally die as well.

CHAPTER
TWENTY-ONE

Megan wiped sweat from her brow for the hundredth time. Her T-shirt clung to her. The stale air made the inescapable cabin feel like a rotting sauna. The creature's hissing had come and gone all day, never disappearing for more than a few minutes. The cabin shook periodically, perhaps from the swaying branches pushing against the roof and gables when the monstrosity passed overhead.

The quiet times felt like a silent countdown until the arachnid's next appearance.

At the moment, the hiss was low, like a punctured bike tire. Megan crawled to the edge of the cabinet and peered into the paper-thin crack between its back and the filthy window. Dusk was fading, meaning they'd been here for nearly twelve hours.

She checked her watch's luminous hands. Thirteen hours. And still no sign of a search party.

Perhaps only a half hour left before full darkness.

Megan turned and moved back on her hands and knees, past a few items they had collected while searching the cabin. Some were potentially useful, others not so much. A pitchfork. A scythe. Some frayed rope that looked as if it wouldn't hold the weight of a child. Two small powder kegs—surely useless after two centuries. Vargas had placed on the pile a flintlock pistol, whose utility Megan also very much doubted. The commemorative Civil War cannons in Riverside Park had a better chance of firing.

"See anything?" Ryan asked.

"It'll be dark soon." Megan focused her beam on the center of the cabin, between where Emma, Ryan, and Vargas had sat. "How much food and water have we got left?"

"We're nearly out of water," Emma said. "Food to last a few more days."

"Never thought we'd be short of water here," Ryan added mournfully. "Any volunteers for a run to the river?"

Vargas dipped a hand inside his plastic bag and produced two cans. "Got some White Claw if that helps."

Megan smiled. "I'm sure we'll bust those open soon."

"And when we run out of everything?" Emma said to the group. "What do we do then? I mean, shouldn't we take our chances while we still have strength?"

"We're not close to that yet," Megan replied. "We seem to still be safe in here. Let's give it a few more hours for help to arrive. If nobody shows, we make a break for it at sunup."

The group murmured in agreement.

Megan had already imagined the scenario in her head. The

group running out of supplies while still trapped. The maddening sound of the nearby stream and distant rapids, taunting them. Luring them to life-giving water—and probably to their deaths.

Someone would eventually lose their shit and make a stupid move.

The hissing reminded everyone of the risk, but they had outrun the beast once before. If it came to it, they simply would have to do it again. But they needed to wait till they had some kind of advantage. Rizzo's capture, as much as she hated the thought, had given them time to beat the arachnid to the cabin.

Or maybe they hadn't escaped. Perhaps this was exactly where it wanted them. Farther from the road. Deeper into its killing zone . . .

Megan shuddered at the thought.

They emptied all their food onto a groundsheet. Emma and Ryan had brought freeze-dried supplies, which, of course, needed water. Vargas had a few ramen noodle cups. Again, just add water.

Megan had a plastic bag filled with peanut butter protein snacks—Ethan's favorite healthy food and now, potentially, their lifeline.

They had a few snacks and a few sips of water and went back to silently listening. Megan had tried to gain an appreciation of the creature's movements in relation to the cabin. This had proved impossible because it had always seemed to come in from a random direction. No pattern. They weren't dealing with a creature of habit, with a methodical hunting routine.

Trying to work out the potential behavior of a terrifying unknown species struck her as one of the weirdest things she had ever done. All she could do was fall back on her operational skills.

Even the world's leading arachnologists would find this situation baffling.

For the next twenty minutes, no one said a word. At each

of the creature's comings and goings, they exchanged nervous glances, their faces dim in the beam's peripheral light.

Twenty minutes later, during a moment when the hissing had waned, a new sound rose above the faint roar of the distant rapids.

"You hear that? It sounds like a guy's voice," Ryan said. "I'm sure of it."

Everyone quickly shuffled toward the barricaded door.

Nothing immediately followed. Megan refused to believe this was a sign of help. Since the disaster a year ago, she had learned to expect the worst.

"If it's a dude," Vargas said, "he's not gonna last a second out there alone."

"Shut up and listen," Emma snapped.

A cry joined the noise of the hissing and the rapids.

"There it is again," Ryan said.

To Megan, it sounded like a wail of desperation rather than a call from a search party. She kept that thought to herself for the moment. It wasn't inconceivable that another poor soul had fallen into the arachnid's clutches.

"*Help . . . me,*" a man's voice carried faintly through the forest.

"What the . . . ?" Emma said. She strained to listen more closely.

A few moments later, the voice from the forest came again. "*Help . . . me . . .*"

"That sounds like . . . my dad."

Ryan shook his head. "I don't think that's him, babe. You saw what happened earlier."

"Just listen goddamn it. I know what my father sounds like!"

Emma moved her ear closer to the wall. Ryan moved protectively by her side.

Megan understood why Emma would want to believe that it was her father calling out. More than once, she had found herself waking up at home, expecting Mike and Ethan to walk through the door. A floorboard creaked at night—Ethan coming to her bedroom after suffering a nightmare. Something clicked downstairs—Mike in his office. As if her personal tragedy had all been a bad dream.

She wished.

But just like the state fair, this nightmare was real.

"*Emma! Ryan! Can anyone hear me?*" the voice called.

"IT'S DAD! He's alive!" Emma scrambled to her feet. "We need to do something. Now!"

Ryan sprang up beside her.

Vargas had frozen with an unlit cigarette inches from his lips. He remained quiet, eyes darting back and forth between the two.

Megan had recognized Rizzo's voice the second time he called out. She had no reason to doubt he was still alive, but she needed time to process the implications. Her first reaction was shock mixed with relief. The next thought: *Is this a trap?*

"*Richard! Megan! If you can hear me, please help.*"

Shortly after the last cry, the hissing stopped. Almost as if the arachnid wanted them to hear the pastor's next cries and be drawn outside.

"He sounds in pain," Emma said. "We can't just leave him out there!"

"The hell we can't," Vargas said. "It would be madness to go out there."

"*Anyone! Please!*" Rizzo yelled.

Emma turned toward Megan and Vargas. "I'm not leaving my dad out there to die. Stay here if you want. I'm going out."

She put her hands on the barricade.

"Wait a second," Megan replied. "Let's think this through first. It could be some kind of trap!"

Emma ignored her and threw a tea crate to one side. Ryan also began pulling away the objects they had stacked behind the table. Within a minute, they had just about cleared a way out.

"Wait!" Vargas bellowed. "That thing might be waiting behind the closest tree. Who knows what the fuck is going on!"

He tried halfheartedly to stop them, but Ryan pushed him hard and continued tearing the last of the barricade apart.

Megan couldn't criticize them for risking everyone's safety. She thought back to the moment her family died. How she recoiled from the intense heat of the fire consuming their bodies, and couldn't unlock the pin to free her husband and son.

In hindsight, she would gladly have burned half her body if it meant saving them. So she couldn't blame Emma for taking this shot. If anything, she admired her for it, because the prospect of dying out there was real, never mind Rizzo's apparent survival.

And that death could come the moment they opened the door.

Emma and Ryan pulled aside the last crate of the barricade, pushed the cabin door open, and ran out into the night.

CHAPTER

TWENTY-TWO

"Fuck . . . me," Vargas said as he watched Emma and Ryan bolt out of the cabin. He stooped down and quickly grabbed the antique pitchfork. Its weathered hickory handle and four rusty tines were better than nothing.

They weren't thinking straight. Allowing their emotions to override their good sense.

And he was not dying because of them.

Vargas looked out the open cabin door as Emma and Ryan ran into dark woods. The hissing continued maybe a hundred yards away, adding to the sinister, doom-ridden atmosphere. Trees casting dark shadows across the ground. The creak of branches in the pitch-black canopy.

A minor consolation was the cool evening air now flooding into the cabin.

At any moment, he expected the canopy to thrash, and the monstrous creature to close in on them at high speed. This was probably what the damned thing had been waiting for all along. Rizzo was just the bait.

The last thought brought him to an obvious conclusion.

"I'm telling you, this has gotta be a trap!" Vargas shouted out the door.

"I agree," Megan said.

"Stop, goddamn it!"

The couple outside scanned about with their flashlights, as if trying to decide which path to take. In the cabin, it had been impossible to ascertain the direction of Rizzo's cries. It had also been impossible to get an idea of the arachnid's location.

"*Help me!*" Rizzo pleaded in the distance, his voice cracking.

Emma and Ryan both looked in the direction of the campsite.

"That way!" Ryan shouted.

They took off immediately, and within seconds the darkness swallowed them.

"It's suicide," Vargas said, rocking on his heels by the door.

The hissing continued softly. The arachnid had not come for them even after the noise the couple created dismantling the barricade. Surely, though, that was only a matter of time.

"You may be right," Megan said. "But we can't let them go alone, Ricky."

She grabbed the only flashlight left in the cabin: her high-powered UV light. She flicked it on and pointed its beam into the forest, directly on the backs of Ryan and Emma.

Vargas inhaled sharply at the sight. "Oh, my God . . ."

Megan stood rigid for a moment, taking in the shocking view.

The forest, illuminated by UV light for the first time, glowed blue in all directions around Emma and Ryan. Light-blue luminous threads surrounded them, connected between trees, branches, and rocks in a sort of fence, as if the creature had spun a cage of webs around the cabin.

"DON'T MOVE!" Megan bellowed.

The alarm in her voice had the desired effect.

Ryan and Emma stopped dead in their tracks, seeing the threads around their bodies for the first time. They looked over their shoulders toward the cabin, then to their sides at the thousands of luminous fibers spread through the forest in all directions.

Emma's boot was only millimeters from breaking one of the filaments. She stared down at it, frozen in terror.

Ryan shined his flashlight, but the webs all but disappeared under normal light.

Megan flashed her beam out into the dark forest, lighting up thousands more blue webs.

"Don't move a muscle!" Megan followed up. "Very slowly, back up right now!"

She angled the UV beam down at Ryan's and Megan's boots, lighting a path for them to make their way back to the cabin.

The couple slowly backtracked, careful to avoid any of the webs. The terrifying sight all around them seemed to have dampened their motivation to rescue Pastor Rizzo.

Vargas stared, dumbstruck.

They were being systematically hunted from all sides.

CHAPTER

TWENTY-THREE

Megan edged toward the cabin entrance. The sight of thousands of glowing blue webs throughout the forest had turned her legs to lead. She took small, uncertain steps, staring in horror at the tightly woven network. The webs were everywhere, crisscrossing from tree to tree—deadly trip wires strung in all directions.

The monster had been busy surrounding them.

Or had the webs always been here?

Vargas, pitchfork in hand, matched her stride, retreating back into the cabin.

The more she got to know him, the more similar she realized they were. He, too, knew that if they wanted to stay alive, they had to start properly assessing the situation *before* acting.

The cabin that had bought them some temporary safety now turned out to be a trap. And the only way out was to negotiate a seemingly impassable network of webs likely designed to ensure their capture.

They reentered the cabin and moved to either side of the doorway. She kept her beam focused on a path for Ryan and Emma, helping them make it back without disturbing the arachnid's trap. Both stayed rooted to the spot, scanning their immediate vicinity.

"Back up," Megan snapped. "Right now."

They would be mad to keep going after seeing this. The only sensible option was to return.

Finally, the couple slowly crept back. Their saving grace, perhaps, was the small clearing around the cabin. Two trees deep into the forest, they had stopped only inches from snapping a web.

In the distance, Pastor Rizzo's agonized voice cried out one last time.

Emma stopped in midstride. The look on her face matched the anguish in her father's voice. Ryan stood close by her side. He spun in the direction of the campsite.

Megan hoped Emma wouldn't turn and run. She couldn't comprehend the exact nature of the luminous threads. They didn't look like anything she had ever seen before. It was already clear they were dealing with an unknown enemy, and this only complicated their already daunting problem.

To her great relief, Ryan grabbed Emma's arm and eased her forward. She didn't require much encouragement, and they both returned to the cabin, defeated.

All four peered back out as Megan played her beam across a different stand of trees, highlighting thousands more webs. The taut lines, spun at ankle, waist, and chest heights, sent a chill down her spine.

Methodical. Designed to catch prey no matter its height.

But the hissing remained distant.

"What the hell is going on?" Ryan said breathlessly.

"Isn't it obvious?" Vargas replied. "That damned monster has us surrounded by its web. We get trapped in it, and we're spider food."

"I don't think so," Megan said. "Otherwise, it would have attacked Emma and Ryan just now. But it's nowhere near us at the moment. Why?"

"Maybe it's busy feasting on a bear," Vargas said.

"Not only that, but we're not truly trapped," Megan added, studying the network of spun threads. "I mean, we can break through those webs easily. They aren't dense enough or strong enough to stop us. So they must be for something else."

"To scare the shit out of us until it comes back for seconds," Vargas said.

"No," Megan said. "Think."

Everyone stood in silence.

"It's the vibration."

"What do you mean?" Emma said.

"They're like trip wires," Megan added. "Break a web; that thing can track us. No matter where we go."

"You can't be serious," Ryan said.

"Yo, she's right," Vargas replied. "I seen *Animal Planet.* Spiders can't see for shit. But touch one of their webs, they know you're there. Spider sense, right?"

"Exactly," Megan replied.

"You've gotta be shitting me," Ryan said. "So we break those lines, it comes hunting?"

"We don't know for certain, but it makes the most logical sense," Megan replied. "Think about it. We probably broke through hundreds of trip lines when we ran from the clearing. That's how it followed us here. But when we stopped running and hid in the cabin, it could no longer find us and moved on."

An unsettling thought occurred to her. She shined her flashlight beam across the cabin and played it on the skeleton. Sure enough, the tightly woven threads around the bones glowed bright blue. At some stage, the arachnid had entered here—when it was much smaller and could fit through the door.

Ryan shined his beam down, too, and again the webs became invisible.

"What the actual fuck," he muttered. "Why does yours work?"

"It's the UV light," Megan said.

"Meaning?"

"My husband bought it for spotting scorpions during our camping trips. Must be the chemicals in the webs. You can hardly see the webs with a regular beam, but this baby lights them up with ultraviolet. Probably best to save the batteries." She killed the light, leaving Ryan's flashlight to illuminate the cabin's decaying floorboards and walls.

"Wait," said Emma. "So if that ultraviolet light can show us where the webs are, can't we just trace a path toward my dad? We can't just leave him out there to die."

"I had a thought about that," Megan said.

She took a deep breath, barely believing what she was about to suggest.

"I'll climb onto the roof with the UV light. Let's see what we're really dealing with here."

"Yeah, find us a way to the goddamn bus," Vargas said.

"Dad first," Emma demanded.

Vargas pursed his lips. His eyes narrowed. It appeared obvious that he wanted to disagree, but something held him back. Maybe it was his previous relationship with Emma. Or perhaps he had some goodness inside him that had finally snapped free of his restraints.

"Let's have a look first," Megan replied. "No point arguing about hypotheticals yet. Ricky, can you give me a hand?"

"You think the roof'll hold?"

"You calling me fat?" Megan gave him an icy look, but she couldn't hold it and it dissolved into a grin.

Vargas burst out laughing.

"Make sure you keep on the center beam of the roof," Vargas said, smiling.

"Will do."

"Anything we can do?" Ryan asked.

She shook her head. "Listen for that monster. You hear it come closer, I'll expect you to yank me back in."

"You got it."

Emma stepped closer and said softly, "I'm glad you're here."

Megan smiled.

As she left the cabin, she prayed her idea would be enough to see the surviving members of the group to safety.

Vargas moved to the corner of the cabin and leaned against the wall. He interlaced his fingers, ready to take Megan's boot.

She briefly surveyed the surrounding forest. Leaves rustled, partially muffling the distant hiss. Moonlight streamed through gaps in the canopy, highlighting patches of the gently swaying undergrowth.

But Megan saw no sign of movement anywhere around them.

She shuddered at the thought of the now invisible webs, waiting to alert the arachnid of their movements. It made sense to her how Rizzo, DeLuca, and the family had all been taken from different parts of the forest, apparently by the same creature. It had its own natural tracking system.

"I haven't got all night," Vargas said—clearly tongue in cheek, though his words carried the truth.

Megan slipped her flashlight into her thigh pocket, planted her boot on his hands, and thrust upward. She grasped the top of the solid wooden beam and hauled herself up. Those pull-ups in the gym during her sabbatical were finally paying off.

She shuffled onto the roof, keeping herself flat to spread her weight out, and crawled up to the ridge.

From up here, nearly twenty feet above the ground, she had an excellent all-around view under the starry sky. To her left and right, the forest swept downhill—one way leading to the bus, the other to the campsite and the fierce rapids.

At any other time, this vantage point would have given her a perfect moment, one she'd loved to share with Mike and Ethan. She fished her flashlight from her pocket, powered it on, and swept the beam across the treetops and the ground below.

The sight almost took her breath away.

Tens of thousands of luminous webs surrounded the cabin, as expected, and formed another line near the top of the trees. Every time her beam played over the branches, it made that area of the woods glow blue.

Close by, the webs were expectedly thick in density, but they thinned in the direction of the campsite and the river.

She focused her beam on the section of forest that led toward the bus and the road.

In that direction, there seemed to be millions of webs spun everywhere. High and low. Between branches and rocks, in the treetops, even between blackberry brambles.

It was impassable. It was impossible.

There was only one direction they could possibly go.

Megan knew that the others wouldn't like what she had to say.

CHAPTER
TWENTY-FOUR

Megan dropped down from the eaves. Her boots thumped into the damp earth, and she sank to a crouch. She took the opportunity to scan the quiet forest again, keeping her flashlight off.

Nothing moved.

Her hunch had to be right. It was the vibration in the webs that attracted this thing.

Her overriding focus was to not react through fear, as Emma and Ryan had done when almost running straight through a skein of webs.

Vargas grabbed under her armpit and hauled her up. His hand trembled against her biceps as she got to her feet.

She didn't blame him for being terrified. She certainly was.

"Thanks," she said.

"So we gonna live?" he asked.

"Let's get back in the cabin first. Come on."

Megan and Vargas ducked back inside and set about barricading the door once again. Despite the warm evening, the hairs on her arms prickled at the mental image of the trip-wire labyrinth. But she kept a good poker face, serene on the surface while her mind spun furiously. If they wanted to execute a plan together, everyone needed to remain composed.

Emma gave her a look of anticipation. Her father hadn't called out since before Megan climbed onto the roof. Whether he was still alive was very much an open question. But if he was, every minute they left him stranded and exposed was a tick against his staying that way.

Vargas closed the door behind them and slid the bolt home. His action left the beam of Ryan's flashlight angled up toward the ceiling, bathing them all in a pale amber glow.

"So what did you see?" Ryan asked.

"The webs stretched the full range of my flashlight. Tightly packed around the cabin. Easily three times as thick in the direction of the bus. It knows we came in that way, and it set a trap. We can't go that way, no matter what."

"Shit," Vargas replied.

"So what do we do?" Emma asked.

"The webs thin out considerably going toward the campsite. And that's the direction we heard Pastor Rizzo from."

"But that's the wrong goddamn direction," Vargas replied, annoyed. "That takes us deeper into the woods. How about we get to the river and float back to the bus?"

"That's Class V rapids, dumbass," Ryan said. "It'll tear us apart."

"Maybe I'll take my chances, asshole."

"Cool it, guys," Megan snapped. "The campsite is our only possible path. I know it's deeper into the woods, but it's the only way we can go. And we should go *now*."

"Why?" Ryan asked.

"Because of the UV light," Vargas said.

"Exactly," Megan replied. "This ultraviolet light is useless in daytime. We can only see it light up the webs in the dark. So the clock's ticking until sunrise. We head toward the campsite and try and find an alternate way back from there. Or signal for help from the clearing."

The couple nodded in agreement.

"Okay, good. Grab anything we might need from that pile of junk. The sooner we're out of here, the better."

Ryan and Emma walked over the creaking floorboards to the far end and began checking out various tools that might serve as weapons.

"Grab those too," Megan said, pointing to the two small powder kegs on the floor.

"These can't possibly still be good," Ryan said.

"Supposedly, gunpowder lasts for decades or longer if you keep it dry," Megan replied, "and those kegs are still sealed. Better than nothing, right?"

They stowed one keg in Emma's pack, the other in Ryan's, and moved to the door.

Vargas stood, slowly shaking his head.

"Problem?" Megan asked.

"What if we can't find a way back to the bus? What if we can't signal for help? What do we do then?"

"We'll cross that bridge when we come to it," Megan replied. "But no one's going to find us holed up in here, Ricky. That's a fact. We've got to move."

"And another thing," Vargas added. "We aren't entirely sure your theory is accurate."

"You're right," Megan said.

With that, she leaned down and snapped off a weak leg of the table in the center of the room.

"But we can find out."

She turned on her UV light, opened the cabin door, and aimed the beam outward. Her pulse quickened at the thought of her next move. She was inviting danger, but the group had limited options if they wanted to survive.

With all her might, she flung the table leg far into the forest, easily breaking through several webs in the process. The leg crashed through trip lines and disappeared into the undergrowth.

Megan held her breath.

CHAPTER

TWENTY-FIVE

"Why the hell did you do that!" Vargas yelled out.

"Because if I'm right, we'll be safe in here," Megan replied. "That monster tracks vibration, I'm sure of it."

"And if you're wrong, we're all dead," Ryan shot back.

Everyone listened intently, scanning between the trees for signs of movement.

Nothing.

Silence.

They waited another minute or two.

She better be right, Vargas thought to himself.

Then, in the distance, a faint sound.

The unmistakable hissing. Far away, branches cracked

in the treetops. Everyone edged back a few inches from the door.

Ryan grabbed a piece of wood, ready to bash the approaching creature if need be. Vargas took up a fighting stance, brandishing his pitchfork at the door. Megan clutched her little pocketknife in her shaking hand.

Emma leaned close to Megan. "I hope this works, for all our sakes."

"Me too."

In the space of a few seconds, the hissing grew from quiet to deafening. The arachnid was coming, and coming fast.

Birds squawked. Snapped twigs and small branches fell to the forest floor.

Roughly fifty yards into the woods, the canopy thrashed. Then the movement came directly for the cabin.

Nervous anticipation had Vargas more on edge than ever before—more, even, than when he first jacked a truck, or the time he escaped the police by a miracle after robbing a pawn shop.

The hissing built to a level that made his ears hurt. Maybe the creature did this to disorient its victims. He had no idea, and at the moment, he didn't really care. Vargas focused on the thrashing, now clearly visible in the canopy and closing fast on where Megan had thrown the table leg.

The other three stood to Vargas's left, staring out the doorway. It was just his luck that he ended up here with an impulsive hothead and two women who couldn't fight their way out of a paper bag. If he was getting out of this dire situation, it would have to be his doing.

The canopy stopped thrashing. A heartbeat later, the hissing abruptly stopped, and the forest immediately around the cabin fell silent.

What the hell?

The dark shape of the creature dropped from between the branches and scuttled down a tree trunk. The coordinated movement of its thick legs made it look almost mechanical as it descended at alarming speed.

"Jesus Christ," Ryan murmured.

The massive jet-black arachnid shot into the undergrowth, right at the point where the table leg had hit. A few seconds later, it circled the area, rustling the ferns again and again, in an ever-widening spiral.

For a split second, Vargas got a good view of the monster as it raced through a sparse area of brush, its sharp fangs pale in the moonlight.

And the wider the arachnid swept, the nearer it came to the cabin . . .

Vargas expected that sooner or later, it would either slam into the wooden wall or rush straight into the cabin.

The sliver of refuge the structure had given them now felt flimsy and ephemeral. He felt as if they had only delayed the inevitable, living a little longer in fear until the cruel end arrived. Metaphorically, it was like climbing to the highest point on the *Titanic* as the mighty ship slipped into the icy black Atlantic.

He squeezed the pitchfork's weathered haft and tried to regulate his erratic breaths. This time he couldn't blame the cigarettes. He wondered whether anyone would ever see him again—whether anyone would care.

Vargas had no family to grieve him—only acquaintances who would be more than happy to take over his responsibilities on the street.

This sobering thought quickly vanished from his mind as the giant arthropod tore through the forest only twenty yards from the cabin, at twice the speed of an Olympian sprinter. It raced back into the darkness for another circuit. Perhaps the next time it entered the clearing, it would come close enough to sense the group's presence.

He would probably get one shot if the thing attacked.

So better make it count.

In his peripheral vision, Megan slowly took a step back, still gripping her ridiculous little pocketknife. She could probably carve the arachnid a nice toothpick it could use after eating them all. That was about it.

"Don't think your plan is working, boss," he said.

"It will," Megan replied, though without quite the same confident ring as before.

If Vargas had known a prayer, he would be saying it about now. Emma was the only reason he ever dipped his toe into religion in the first place. But right now all that was pointless. No prayer or invocation would save them.

"Shut the door," Ryan demanded.

"Not yet," Megan said. "I'm telling you, it can't sense our presence."

The arachnid closed to within ten yards.

Vargas took another step back. Hooking his boot around a tea crate, he slid it in front of him. It wouldn't shield him for more than a split second, but maybe that would give him the vital moment he needed to stab the thing and flee. That was his best and only plan. He raised the pitchfork, ready to thrust it right under those horrible fangs.

Everyone stayed silent.

The arachnid scuttled past, only a tree or two from the clearing. Its eight spiny legs weaved between the trunks with a nimbleness that defied its size and bulky body.

Emma let out a long, shuddering breath.

"That's it," Ryan growled. "Next time it comes, it'll be right—"

In the darkness only a dozen yards away, the undergrowth stopped moving.

The entire forest surrounding the cabin once again fell silent.

"Holy shit," Vargas murmured to himself.

No one moved.

Had it sensed them? Was it creeping slowly toward the cabin?

Moments later, the arachnid scuttled up a tree trunk and disappeared into the canopy. Then the hissing split the air. At this range, it made Vargas feel as if his head would explode.

But then the racket moved away, diminishing by the second. Going to another part of the forest.

Vargas breathed a heavy sigh of relief. It seemed they were okay for the moment. No one spoke. The others, like him, were no doubt listening for the beast's return.

During this time, they heard nothing from Rizzo. Vargas guessed the old man had said his last amen and was ascending that ghostly escalator toward the pearly gates of heaven.

"Something might've hit a web elsewhere," Megan said, breaking the silence. "So now we know. It can't sense us if we don't disturb one of its webs."

Emma nodded. "Now can we find a way through the tangle to search for my dad?"

"I say we go," said Megan.

"Agreed," Ryan said. "The faster we're out of these woods, the better."

Vargas agreed with the sentiment, though not with the route they were about to take. For now he kept quiet. A moment would come when he could make his break. The timing wasn't right now. He had no UV light, and he needed these people to get clear of the trip lines.

As soon as that happened, Vargas was heading straight for the bus. On his own. Putting these events firmly behind him.

CHAPTER
TWENTY-SIX

Megan stood facing the glowing forest. She rotated the UV light from left to right, searching for the start of the route they hoped would take them to Pastor Rizzo. The luminous webs between trees were roughly one, three, and five feet in height. The thick mesh of webs overhead in the treetops didn't really matter.

She equated this task to when a burglar enters a museum to steal a precious vase, twisting and contorting to avoid the laser beams—the obvious difference being that if someone broke a web, they would quickly face a hell far worse than cops and jail.

Happily, that particular version of hell was hissing somewhere in the direction of the bus. She pictured it clambering through the treetops, hunting some unlucky animal that had sent a vibration down a web, steering the arachnid to its precise location.

The last thought made her shudder.

Megan zipped up her fleece jacket, protecting her neck from the cool night air. She looked over her shoulder.

Vargas stood directly behind her, pitchfork in hand and a steely resolve in his dark eyes. She had no doubt he would fight if they came under attack, though he would probably be fending for himself, given his odd preoccupation with something beyond their situation. He didn't strike her as the altruistic type, but their job right now was to survive, not judge each other as human beings. As long as they stayed together and got through this, nothing else mattered tonight.

Then came Emma, with Ryan at the rear. Both held their packs by their sides. Wearing them wasn't an option while stooping under trip lines.

Behind everyone, the cabin sat secured. If everything should turn to shit in the next few minutes, this was their rendezvous point. After that, she supposed it was a case of fight or die.

"Ready?" Megan asked.

"Can't wait," Vargas replied.

Smart-ass, as usual.

The other two just nodded.

Megan told herself to act with conviction. She already knew the terrible price of stalling or shying away from a dangerous challenge. She walked slowly and carefully to the tree line and their first obstacle. Once they were deep in the forest, there was no chance of running without posting constant location updates to the creature.

She carefully swung her daypack between the bottom two

strands, and it thudded on the leaf-covered ground. Megan hunched down and shined her light on the two filaments. Up close, they looked twice the thickness of an everyday spiderweb, but spaced wide enough to stoop between.

On a normal day. One false move right now would cost everyone's life.

Megan thrust her foot between the webs and planted it on the other side. Satisfied that she wouldn't slip, she ducked through with utmost care.

She turned back toward the group, casting her light on the webs.

Relief washed away the worst of the fear. She hadn't disturbed anything. The webs remained taut and still, glowing softly in her beam.

Megan took a few steps back, keeping the UV beam on the threads so the rest of the group could pass safely through. Vargas slid his pitchfork through, then ducked after it. Ryan and Emma followed, backpacks first. Every few feet, Megan repeated the procedure, and in that fashion they labored slowly through the forest.

The process was exhausting and required seamless concentration. Megan was accustomed to long bouts of intense focus after years at her job. But she worried that other minds—especially Vargas's—would drift.

Within a few minutes, the moonlit cabin had disappeared from view. They had made it past their original path from the bus and were now heading toward the campsite.

The trees were packed tighter as the ground swept down toward the river, meaning smaller spaces to duck between. The undergrowth was denser too. One fern springing against a thread would likely bring the predator. Anyone could do that by accident.

She kept moving forward slowly and methodically, eyeing every blue-lit fiber as they moved through the forest.

They moved into the next cramped space surrounded by webs. Then the next. Like stepping-stones over a boiling pool.

The warmth of the day was gone, but sweat still beaded on her brow. She kept her breathing steady as she crept and crouched through to another small clearing.

Megan took a moment to survey the trees above them. Nothing moved. No hiss announced the creature's presence.

So far, so good. But who could guess what might happen in the next few hours?

The rapids roared louder. A welcoming sound in the dead of night. It meant they were getting closer to their first objective. And possibly closer to Rizzo. Her hope was that he had somehow dragged himself to the campsite, figuring it was a safe space since the creature seemed to live in the trees.

But they hadn't heard from him since the cabin. Maybe half an hour ago.

Once the other three joined her, Megan highlighted another row of trip lines to slip through. A few hundred yards beyond them, the expansive campsite came into view. Clear sky. Rugged mountains behind. No trees.

Emma shuffled her way to Megan's side. "We need to speed up," she said.

"We can't rush this."

"I know. I'm just saying . . ."

"I understand, Emma. You know I'll do my best, but we *must* be careful."

A few more minutes took them to the final grid of glowing threads. She ducked through and ran the UV light over the grass.

No webs.

Megan broke into a fast walk toward the campfire ring—a relief after all the slow, isometric straining from the cabin to here.

The others joined her while she played the beam over the campsite, searching.

No luminous lines.

And no Pastor Rizzo.

Emma's heavy sigh behind her confirmed her last thought. He must still be in the forest somewhere.

"Looks like it's clear," Megan said.

As her beam passed over the remnants of the campsite, Megan caught sight of Connor's tent, which they must have left behind in their hasty morning departure. Something glowed against the inner wall.

"Holy shit!" Vargas said. He edged back a couple of paces.

"Keep your cool, Ricky," Megan said. "It's too small for the creature to fit inside."

"But not your dad," Ryan said. Emma shot him a concerned glance.

Megan crept toward the tent, keeping her light focused on the wall. The others followed. As she closed in, the glow became brighter.

Within twenty yards, it was clear that cobwebs lined the tent's sloping walls. A single filament ran from the tent's entrance into the forest.

"So much for being safe here," Vargas said from behind her.

"We need to check inside," she replied.

"Careful," Vargas said. "Who knows what other prehistoric shit lives in this forest."

Megan couldn't rule out the possibility, but she had to look.

She dropped to all fours and crawled closer. The zipper on the door hadn't been fully closed. She steeled herself, then shined the light inside.

"Please don't tell me . . ." Emma said, her voice shaking.

"It's empty." Megan scrambled back to her feet. "Your dad must be somewhere else in the woods."

"So let's search. He's close. You all heard him."

"I dunno," Vargas said. "We're safe here until morning. We just stay clear of that web. We light a fire and send out smoke signals or some shit. Or we flag down some asshole kayaker as they go by."

"You really are a piece of work, Ricky," Ryan said. "First of all, we don't know if anybody even runs this river. Second, are you really going to wait here while Pastor Rizzo dies?"

Ryan stepped closer. Aggressive. Scowling. This was the angry mechanic from the start of the journey.

"Cool your jets, amigo. Just spitballing ideas."

Ryan stepped closer to Vargas. For the third time, Megan stepped between the two men. "Guys, let's not go down this rathole again. I'm sorry, but Ricky is right on this. The smartest thing to do is light an SOS fire and wait for help. We are safer here, and we don't know where to begin looking."

"Damn right," Vargas added. "In the forest, there's a million ways to get caught. Here, we're cool as long as we don't hit that web going from the tent."

"You realize that means the creature has been here too, right?" Ryan said. "It could hunt us out here in the open too. We're not safe anywhere."

Vargas remained silent, returning Ryan's cold stare.

Emma grabbed Ryan's arm and eased him away. This move seemed to calm him, though he was a long way from relaxed.

"She's right, Ryan," Emma said with a sigh.

"Let's collect as much firewood as we can," Megan said. "Just be very careful not to disturb that web."

The group spread out, gathering fallen limbs and breaking off dead branches and roots. Megan worked her way toward the rapids, with Vargas by her side.

"You need to have patience with Ryan," she said quietly.

"I'm almost out," he replied. "Besides, him and me—we don't want the same things."

"Do *we* want the same things, Ricky?" Megan asked pointedly. Vargas looked away.

Megan picked up bunches of sticks and pine straw they could use as kindling for the fire. She placed them in the fire ring, far enough away from the tent that she wouldn't accidentally break the web. The others followed suit, adding to the pile.

Suddenly, the anguished voice of Pastor Rizzo cried out. And he sounded close by. Maybe only a few minutes into the forest.

"*For God's sake,*" the pastor yelled. "*Anybody. Please!*"

"That's him!" Emma cried out. "He's that way!" She pointed at the far end of the clearing, and she and Ryan grabbed their backpacks.

"Emma, wait!" Megan shouted. She snatched up the UV light and her backpack. "Follow me, everyone. Be very careful!"

Megan moved ahead of everyone and faced the woods.

Ryan and Emma followed closely as she flicked on the ultraviolet light, illuminating thousands more webs in the forest, in the direction of Pastor Rizzo's voice. She took her first cautious step into the woods.

But Vargas hung back.

Megan turned and looked directly at him.

"Ricky?"

"Yeah, you guys go ahead," he replied. "I'll be fine right here, thanks."

"Are you *serious?*"

He peered up and locked eyes with Megan. Her eyes rolled with disappointment and resignation. Vargas looked down at the ground but didn't move an inch.

"Fine. Stay," Megan replied. "Get that fire lit."

With that, she turned and took a few steps deeper into the woods.

Then she froze.

She swung her flashlight down. There in the ferns, a web had stretched across the small space between two green stems.

Her mouth hung open, but no words came. The arachnid had spun its trap across the ground too. They had been lucky so far, but that luck may have just run out.

A single web had bowed against her shin but remained unbroken. The slightest added tension could snap it.

But even this much disturbance may already have done the job . . .

"Guys . . ." she whispered loudly.

"Holy shit," Emma said, staring down.

"What?" Ryan squinted as he stared into the ferns and saw the web against the shin of Megan's pant leg.

"Jesus Christ," he murmured. "Megan . . . don't move."

CHAPTER
TWENTY-SEVEN

Megan tried to dial back the fear that gripped her, and to ignore
the urge to sprint for her life. Emma and Ryan stared at her, terri
fied the arachnid would soon be upon them.

Vargas was bending down, trying to light the kindling in the
fire ring. As the pine straw caught and the bigger sticks began to
burn, he looked at the group in the distance. They stood motionless a few steps into the tree line.

"Hey! What the hell's going on?" he yelled.

No reply.

He snatched up the pitchfork and ran to the edge of the forest,
where he took in the group's situation.

Sweat trickled down Megan's face. The web was bent taut around her pant leg but had not broken. Yet.

The group listened intently for any sound that the creature was on its way. They heard only crickets and night birds.

Megan finally said, "I'm gonna try and pull my leg away . . ."

She gingerly drew her leg back, terrified the web would stick to her pants and break. As she pulled back, the filament clung to the fabric, then twanged taut again.

Could the arachnid sense a vibration so slight? It seemed improbable. But not impossible.

Megan stood still and listened to the forest sounds. Crickets chirring and a couple of katydids clicking. A screech owl.

The other three stared upward. All waited for the distant hiss, growing in volume.

Megan frantically scanned the canopy. She winced at the creak of a branch. Turned at the breath of wind sighing through the forest.

But no hissing.

Then an odd stench invaded her nostrils. A mix of dirt and rotting meat.

Something moved in her peripheral vision.

Close.

Big.

Within touching distance.

The massive arachnid climbed down a nearby tree trunk, descending silently and smoothly on its horrifying eight legs. Megan turned her head to look at the monstrosity. Its multiple pairs of glittering black eyes, the shudder-inducing fangs. It emitted a low, staccato chatter, like the sound of an old-fashioned typewriter in the hands of an amphetamine-crazed stenographer.

It was less than three feet away.

Not daring to move a muscle, Megan whispered out the side of her mouth, "Everybody, freeze."

Emma turned her head, following Megan's gaze. Seeing the creature, she sucked in a breath.

Before she could scream, Megan reached over and clamped a hand over her mouth.

"It can't see us," Megan said softly. "It senses vibration. Don't move a muscle. We can't outrun it, anyway."

The chitinous exoskeleton gleamed like lacquer as it passed inches from her arm. She stifled the urge to back away, despite being one twitch from brushing against the monster.

It wasn't coming directly for them just yet, though that could change in the blink of an eye.

She stared in horror as the arachnid crawled into the undergrowth, head and body towering over the ferns. It was maybe six feet tall and had to weigh easily six hundred pounds. It stopped by the web that Megan had touched, only a yard from her boots, and palpated it delicately with a foreleg. She tried to will her galloping heart to slow down.

Emma let out a whimper. She had her lips squeezed together. In the moonlight, tears glistened on her cheeks.

Ryan quietly shushed her.

Please, God. Please make it go away.

But Megan knew that praying for divine intervention was not a strategy.

Vargas raised the fork higher. He looked as though he was going to attack the thing. Megan gave him a grimace of disapproval and an emphatic shake of the head. He lowered the fork a few inches.

She couldn't control Vargas's actions. Her only hope was that he saw the sense in not provoking the arachnid while it wasn't coming for them.

The creature sidled to the right. It started methodically around the little glade, like a trapper inspecting his snares. It moved away from her and to within two strides of Vargas.

* * *

Vargas considered his limited options. The other three were like lambs going to the slaughter. Ryan and Emma stood side by side, paralyzed by the arachnid's sudden, silent appearance. Clearly unsure what to do next. But doing nothing was never going to win the day.

Megan was probably trying to figure things out. Problem was, the forest wasn't a boardroom, and the creature wasn't some corporate douchebag.

He should have taken the UV light and made his own way, because one of these jerks was bound to break a web.

Regardless, all he had was here and now. And it was setting up to be a fight to the death with something that had been perfecting its deadly skills for at least the past few centuries. He rated their chances from slim to zip.

The arachnid loomed beside him, moving smoothly along the trip line that Megan had disturbed.

It was clear to Ricky that the creature was blind and likely deaf too. It had yet to detect their presence, even though it was right next to them. Rather, it studied the web, trying to chase down the unexplained disturbance.

Regardless, fight-or-flight was kicking in. To hell with Megan's "strategy"—he had to do something. The nervous energy inside him was ready to erupt. If he could channel that into a lethal strike with the fork . . .

The arachnid turned toward him. Those fangs could slice through him as easily as cutting Jell-O.

Vargas wasn't going out this way, gurgling out his last breath while being dragged like a rag doll through the canopy, his face bouncing off tree limbs, then getting the life sucked out of him until his entire body was a dry husk. No chance. If this eight-legged son of a bitch was taking him down, it would have to do it with a pitchfork buried in its ugly head.

He glanced across to the other three. Megan's silent expression pleaded with him not to move on the arachnid. Ryan and Emma were now also shaking their heads.

Vargas drew in a deep breath. His pulse pounded in his ears. The throbbing stress headache made him blink.

If they didn't want him to attack the thing and save them, was running an option?

The thing continued circling the clearing and moved closer to Ryan and Emma. If it attacked them first, he could use the distraction to reach the river and dive in. Keeping close to the bank, he just might be able to keep from drowning. He could toss the pitchfork toward the others and make a break for it. Of course, this option meant certain death for the other three, though it sure beat *his* certain death.

No, Ricky. You couldn't do that to your worst enemy.

He refocused. Told himself that he controlled his own destiny. He had the ability to get out of this. His hands twitched holding the fork. He readied himself to give it all he had. Sure, it was a one-shot deal, but it was likely their only play.

A hand clamped around his biceps.

"Don't do it," Megan whispered.

Vargas shook free of her grip.

"Just wait," she whispered. "Please."

He drew the pitchfork back, ready to strike.

Screw her plan . . .

A heartbeat later, the arachnid shot away from the glade at high speed. It ran past another skein of webs and dashed around the clearing in a wide arc.

No one moved a muscle or said a word.

And with that, it was gone.

Vargas sank to his knees, gripping the pitchfork to keep his balance. He felt drained, as if the creature had already sucked the life out of him.

* * *

Megan, still shaking, let out a long, unsteady breath. For now it seemed they were safe. But how long they could continue to elude the creature, she didn't know. They had only dodged a bullet launched by her carelessness.

No one spoke or moved while the monster clambered up into the treetops and disappeared from view.

A few minutes later, hissing erupted from a remote part of the forest.

"It didn't see us," Emma blurted.

"Exactly," Megan replied.

"Did you know?"

"It was a calculated guess."

"A damn lucky guess," Vargas replied.

"Yes," Megan admitted. "But if we had run, it would have picked us off immediately."

Vargas gazed at the three of them. "Just make sure there isn't a next time."

"I won't make the same mistake again," Megan replied. "But now we know it can't see or hear us. If we hit a web and stay completely still, we have a chance."

Ryan and Emma nodded.

"Hate to burst your bubble, boss," Vargas interjected, "but we also learned one more thing." He locked eyes with Megan and continued. "That fucker can move silently through these woods without us knowing. It can be anywhere, anytime, and we have no way to track it."

His response chilled her. She hadn't considered this. The arachnid's abrupt appearance out of nowhere had stunned her, but it also laid out in stark relief just how appallingly little they knew of the creature's behavior.

"You're right," Megan finally said.

Vargas looked back toward the campsite. "So what now—"

"*Help me . . .*" Rizzo cried in the distance.

Closer. Weaker. Perhaps near death, though maybe not as close as the four of them had just come. Emma turned toward an area of sparser trees, a hundred yards from the riverbank.

"We continue," Megan said. "But, Ricky . . ."

Vargas eyed her.

"We need your help. *I* need your help."

And she meant it. If the creature came back, if they found any of the missing parishioners, if any one of a hundred other things happened, it was Ricky who had the best gut instinct and survival skills. Their odds, while already slim, were just a bit better with him around.

"Will you help me?" she asked.

Vargas pulled out a half-smoked cigarette from his pack, lit it, and took two more puffs before flicking it to the ground and grinding it out.

He lifted his head and looked at Megan.

"Fuck it. Lead the way, boss."

CHAPTER
TWENTY-EIGHT

The roar of the rapids increased as the four crept along, ducking and contorting their way through the intricate network of webs. Megan looked up every few seconds, aware that the monstrous arachnid could be lurking somewhere nearby. Uncaring stars twinkled here and there between the branches. But the canopy was thick here, shrouding the immediate area in near blackness.

If they couldn't find Rizzo, they needed to get out of these claustrophobic woods. For sooner or later, someone was bound to make a mistake.

The two likely candidates had refrained from doing anything stupid. For the moment. Both Vargas and Ryan were tight-lipped, with all their energy focused on the task of getting past the trip lines.

Everyone glanced in all directions, visibly sharing her unease after the creature's last appearance. And they were potentially heading for one of its known haunts, unless Rizzo had somehow escaped.

After seeing his battered body being dragged through the canopy earlier, Megan considered it unlikely. She trained her UV light ahead of them, trying to identify the clearest route forward.

The pattern of webs changed as they neared a small rocky escarpment by the riverbank—roughly thirty feet high, with vegetation sprouting between the stones. Megan halted before the next webwork of filaments.

The others crowded behind her in another small glade, all of them staring thirty feet ahead.

The thousands—perhaps millions—of fibers stretching from the forest drew closer together as they ran to the foot of the escarpment, eventually converging a few yards ahead to form a glowing, blue cable as thick as a tree trunk. It disappeared into a pitch-black opening in the rock.

Megan shined the UV light all around the cave's mouth, confirming her hunch. No fine threads, no tricky trip wires. Plenty of room to walk around, and no trees.

"I think we found the creature's lair," Megan said. "All the webs converge into that huge cable. It must be able to sit in that one spot and sense the vibrations from millions of webs throughout the forest."

"You think the pastor is down there?" Ryan whispered.

"It's where Dad's voice came from," Emma replied.

"And you want to waltz right in and get him?" Vargas asked. "That's wack."

"Would you go if it was your father?" Ryan shot back.

"Never knew him."

"There's a surprise."

"Stop it," Megan snapped. "Let's listen and observe for a bit."

For the next several minutes, they watched in silence.

Nothing moved around the cave entrance. No hissing, although, as they had learned, this didn't mean much. Megan pondered throwing something into the woods behind them to draw the arachnid out.

If it's even in there.

She quickly discounted the idea—they might not be as lucky during its next search of the disturbed area.

Megan turned to face everyone. "Anybody got any smart ideas?"

"Yeah," Vargas said. "We follow the river right here back to the bus. If the spider catches us chilling here in its living room, we're breakfast."

"We have to see if my father is alive, Ricky!" Emma pleaded.

Ryan said, "We come all this way for you to chicken out?"

"You wanna stomp on a hornet's nest, knock yourself out, sport. Enough of this. I'm getting the fuck outta here."

"Jesus," Ryan growled. "Do you give a shit about anything other than yourself?"

Vargas replied in a sarcastic tone, "You run your mouth a lot, but that's all it ever is. If you feel frisky, lead the way, pal. Jump in that cave headfirst; let us know what you see."

Seeing the two men glare at each other, Megan felt like giving both of them a good, hard slap. The situation demanded every-one's complete cooperation—not this.

"Stop it!" Emma snapped. "We can take a look without touching the line of webs. I mean, we got this far okay, didn't we?"

Megan nodded. "She's right. This is the wrong time to bail on everybody, Ricky."

Vargas stood defiantly and secured his backpack.

"I wish you all the absolute best of luck. I'll take my chances along the river. See you back in the Bronx . . . or not."

And with that, he turned to walk away along the river's edge.

Ryan sprang to his feet and rammed his shoulder into Vargas's back. The two men went sprawling onto the rocky bank of the white water. They came up swinging, their punches connecting with dull thuds.

It seemed unbelievable that they had started a fight, putting everyone's life at risk at the very point when they could be *saving* a life.

"Stop it!" Emma shouted. "Ryan! Ricky! Are you two crazy?" She ran to the edge of the river.

Megan trained her light on the brawling idiots at the water's edge.

Vargas crashed his forehead into Ryan's face. Ryan responded by sinking his teeth into his opponent's arm.

Vargas screamed and thrashed. Ryan swung another punch into the side of his head, though Megan couldn't hear it over the roaring rapids.

Vargas spun and wrapped him in a headlock. Ryan threw his body weight backward, making Vargas smash into Emma, knocking her over into the watercress on the bank.

The men fell into a shallow eddy, where they fought the foaming current and staggered back onto their feet. The river was black in this light and louder than a football stadium full of screaming fans.

Emma sat up, dazed by the blow. "STOP IT!" she begged. "You'll get us all killed!"

The men ignored her pleas and kept swinging at each other in the knee-deep water while also fighting the torrential current.

"STOP IT RIGHT NOW!" Megan shouted.

It was nearly impossible for the men to keep their footing. Vargas let go and kicked Ryan away. But the force of the kick made Vargas stagger, and down he went. He fell backward, head downriver, and fetched up against a rock. He climbed back to his feet, putting his back to the rock to keep upright.

"Are you happy now?" Emma cried from where she had fallen in the watercress. "My dad is in that cave, our friends are in that cave, needing our help, and you dumb shits are fighting like fucking children!"

Ryan took a lurching step toward shore, reaching out to help Emma to her feet. She held out her hand toward him.

Before their hands met, something crashed in the undergrowth.

Megan stiffened.

Emma looked over her shoulder and opened her mouth to scream.

Eight black legs appeared over the top of her.

Before Ryan could clamber ashore and reach her hand, Emma's body shot back toward the thick vegetation. She pulled up two fistfuls of watercress in a futile attempt to keep from being dragged away.

It was no use.

Within a heartbeat, her body vanished from view, snatched away by the monster.

A few seconds later, her garbled screams rang through the forest.

Megan and Vargas stared in shock. It all had happened in the span of perhaps three seconds. Megan turned her gaze toward the burrow in the side of the mountain.

The creature scuttled past the thick cable, with Emma writhing in its mouth, and disappeared into the pitch-black cave.

"EMMA!" Ryan cried out, still struggling not to get swept downriver. "NO!"

But she was gone.

CHAPTER

TWENTY-NINE

Vargas stared, dumbstruck by what he had just witnessed. His upper arm throbbed from when the fight had turned dirty. Ryan stood a few yards upriver, struggling to maintain his balance in the treacherous current, although the eddy was calmer there. His stubborn rage had probably cost the life of his girlfriend, the woman whom Vargas considered "the one who got away."

In any other situation, he would knock ten shades of shit out of the asshole. But they didn't have time for that right now. It could wait till tomorrow—if they survived that long.

Vargas took a few long, deep breaths to calm himself. The current had him pinned against a rock the size of an SUV, and his back ached from repeatedly bashing into it. He tried to step away from the rock and nearly got whisked away. He dug his fingers into a crack and held on for dear life.

His options seemed clear enough: make it to shore and get killed by the monster, or stay here and drown.

At the top of the eddy, Ryan struggled toward shore.

"Emma, no!" he cried again.

Even though Vargas was barely a dozen feet away, he had scant chance of helping Ryan escape the river. He had to find his own way out first.

Think, goddamn it.

Back pressed against the rock, Vargas looked around him. If he shifted right, the current would whip him away and he'd be a dead man. The shore lay to his left—tantalizingly close, but a whirlpool separated him from the river's edge. If he got caught in that, it might keep him under for an hour then spit him out for the crows and coyotes downstream.

He looked upriver toward Ryan. Fighting the current seemed an impossibility, but the water was calmer up there.

If he could work his way up, he might have a fighting chance.

The raging water seemed to hold him against the rock with one hand while pounding him with the other. And eventually, a surge to one side or the other would dislodge him. He couldn't stay here long.

Vargas looked upstream, beyond Ryan. Another twenty feet upstream, a massive log sped through the rapids, coming right toward the man.

Ryan hadn't spotted it.

Vargas hated the guy, but still . . .

"Ryan!" Vargas shouted. "Watch out!"

Ryan turned to look upriver, but too late. The log slammed into his chest, knocking him off his feet. His body went under, and the log jammed itself squarely between two rocks, pinning him completely underwater.

"Fuck!" Vargas shouted. He used all his might to fight the current and reach the log up ahead.

"Megan, help me!"

Wasting no time, she leaped into the eddy where Ryan was, and tried to move the stuck log. Its sheer mass, compounded by the tremendous force of the river, made it impossible to budge.

Fighting the current with all his strength, Vargas took a step upstream, then another. The current pushed and tugged against his legs, twice nearly toppling him, but he fought it, and moments later, he reached the log.

Ryan was completely underwater, wedged between the log and the rocks below. His arms flailed frantically.

Ricky planted his feet against the boulder behind him and pushed with everything he had.

Nothing.

"Push, on three!" Vargas shouted. "One . . . two . . . three!"

Megan and Ricky strained to budge the log.

"It's not gonna work!" Megan shouted.

Vargas thought he heard a muffled shout. "Get his head above water!"

They grabbed Ryan's shoulders and tried to lift his head. His body inched up a tiny bit, but he was still several inches below the surface.

Ryan stared up at them in desperation. He had been underwater for almost a minute.

"LIFT!" Ricky shouted.

They pulled as hard as they could.

Nothing.

Ricky grew frantic, trying to rock the log out of position. Nothing worked.

Ryan's body began to convulse underwater. His shoulders jerked. His single flailing arm began to slow. He was drowning, breathing river water deep into his lungs. His brain and body were being starved of air, only two inches below the surface.

"NO, NO, NO!" Megan cried out.

After one final convulsion, Ryan's body relaxed.

His dead eyes, still wide open, stared up at the surface, looking for a salvation that would never come.

CHAPTER
THIRTY

Tears streamed down Megan's cheeks as the river ran smoothly over Ryan's face. Screaming out an anguished, primal howl, she staggered back onto dry land. She sank onto all fours and slumped against a rock.

As helpless as last year . . .

She had never felt so entrapped in such a wide-open space. They still had hours of darkness until daybreak. A long time to survive between a deadly river and an even deadlier enemy.

Vargas staggered onto land and slumped down beside her, gasping for breath. He dug his cigarettes out of his pocket. The pack was crushed and soaking wet. He flipped open the water-logged lid, then let out an exasperated groan.

The two sat in silence, side by side, backs against a rock, for several long minutes.

There were no words to speak.

Eventually, Vargas broke the silence. "You okay?"

Megan glanced up at him and studied his expression for a moment. He was looking attentively at her.

She dropped her head, lost in thought.

"Last year . . ." she said, struggling to form the words she was about to say. "Last year . . . when Mike and Ethan were trapped in that burning chair . . ."

Her eyes welled up with tears. "There was a moment—a second or two, maybe—when . . . when I could have saved them."

Vargas sat up straight. He appeared taken aback by her admission.

She continued, tears streaming down her face. "There was a locking pin I could have reached—I *should* have reached—but instead I pulled back from the flames. Out of fear, selfishness. I betrayed them. I betrayed myself. And now I live with this constant reminder of what I failed to do . . ."

Megan rubbed her hand along the shiny burn scar on her arm. "Ryan had the same look in his eyes that they did that day. Desperation. Helplessness."

Vargas looked up at her with sympathetic eyes, his trademark streetwise attitude gone.

"I just feel very—"

"I know how you feel," he interjected, losing the tough-guy exterior. "Alone."

She nodded.

"I've been alone all my life," he confessed.

For the first time in the past two days, Megan finally felt

that she was speaking with the real Ricky rather than his cocky persona.

"Don't know what's worse," Vargas said. "Having everything and losing it all, or never having anything to lose."

She couldn't decide either.

The two sat there, staring forward at the wild river, lost in their own thoughts.

"Can I ask you something?" Megan said.

"Shoot."

"What's in the bus?"

Vargas looked up at her, clearly feigning innocence. "I'm not sure what you mean."

"You know exactly what I mean, Ricky. You didn't come here to get away from the city. You left the campsite to go back to that bus. You've been itching to get back there for two days now. So no more bullshitting. I mean, it's not your insulin. That was horseshit. What's on that bus that you're not telling me about?"

Vargas kept staring at the roaring white water. Finally, he turned back and faced her. "About half a million dollars of heroin—street value. Just transporting it to some buyers in West Virginia, and no cop pulls over a church bus full of old people to look for H."

"Got it," Megan replied, unable to hide the disappointment on her face.

Vargas shifted uncomfortably.

"I've got to go back in that cave for them, Ricky," she finally said.

"Yeah, I know you do."

"And I know you're not gonna join me. I won't try and persuade you, but *I've* got to try. You understand?"

"Yeah, I underst—"

***

Before Vargas could finish his sentence, Megan made an odd choking sound.

He turned toward her just as her UV flashlight thudded against the ground and her legs rocketed up toward the canopy.

The arachnid had its front two legs wrapped around Megan and had sunk one of its fangs into her shoulder.

She let out a scream that quickly faded as her body went limp.

A heartbeat later, the creature disappeared with her into the treetops.

Vargas dived for the flashlight and shined it upward. His hands shook as he scanned the branches, fearing the worst. He backed toward the river until the cold water chilled his ankles.

Megan was gone.

Everyone was gone.

Vargas screamed with all his might, and his voice echoed through the canyon.

He shined the UV light through the trees and toward the entrance to the creature's forbidding lair.

Then he looked at the raging torrent behind him—his only possible escape from this hell.

CHAPTER

THIRTY-ONE

Branches whipped against Megan's face. One of the arachnid's front legs had wrapped so tightly around her torso, she could hardly breathe. Twenty feet below, the ground rushed past. Blurry and dark.

A fang had punctured her back just after the arachnid dragged her up a tree trunk. Already, her vision was foggy and all power seemed to drain from her limbs. She tried to scream but managed only a soft whine. Tried to wriggle but couldn't move.

No amount of strategizing would spare her from this fate. Even without being paralyzed by whatever the creature had injected into her, she would have stood no chance.

The thing scuttled at breakneck speed toward the burrow,

letting branches and twigs lash its paralyzed prey along the way. And even though her limbs were immobile, Megan still felt every gasp-inducing hit to her legs, arms, body, and head. Her lower lip swelled. Blood ran from her forehead and pooled in her left eye. She felt searing pain all over.

She blinked, trying to keep her focus. Perhaps to stay present for her terrifying last moments alive. Perhaps this was karma for backing away from the stuck swing chair a year ago. Every member of her family dying with the same desperate look in their eyes.

The speed through the trees slowed as she approached the clearing. She could see only a few feet ahead, but it was enough for her to realize that the arachnid was taking her down a tree, past the escarpment near the river's edge, and toward the cave's mouth.

Drawing in strained breaths, she ransacked her mind for anything that might help. She knew that short of a miracle, she was dead.

The edge of the burrow's entrance rushed toward her face.

She squeezed her eyes shut a second before impact.

* * *

Megan came to with a splitting headache, not knowing how much time had passed. Her whole body throbbed. For a second, she wondered whether she had dreamed it all. Maybe she would wake back up in the Bronx, before this trip ever began. Or, even better, wake up a year earlier when Mike and Ethan were still alive . . .

Then the terrifying reality appeared firmly in her mind's eye.

Her eyes slammed open.

Thousands of webs surrounded her, spun from her knees to

her shoulders. She gasped. Strength was finally returning to her pained limbs, but it didn't matter—she was cocooned tightly from the shoulders down.

Trapped.

She peered up into the cavernous burrow. In the thin moonlight from the opening, it looked maybe three stories high, though the ceiling of fractured rock was barely visible.

"Megan," rasped a voice beside her.

Pastor Rizzo.

She forced her head a few inches to the left. Her vision was still impaired, but she could recognize the blurred outline of the pastor's face. He lay facing her. A string of blood hung from his lip.

"Is that you?" He sucked in a shaky breath.

"It's me, Pastor," she replied.

"My God it hurts," Rizzo groaned.

Her heart broke at the sound of the man. If there was a hell, this was it.

"Is help coming, Megan?" Rizzo asked. His croaking voice echoed in the burrow.

"I don't think so, Pastor."

A dark figure moved behind him, bobbing slowly up and down—surely the arachnid, though she couldn't quite make it out in the darkness.

Now they all were at the monster's mercy, except Vargas. She hoped he would find his way out of this forest alive, but even if he did, there was little hope of any rescue arriving on time.

Megan tried to reach for the penknife in her pocket. Only inches away from her fingers. It was no use. She had been firmly immobilized, prepared for consumption.

She gulped back a cry.

Then Rizzo came into focus.

He grimaced, showing his bloodstained teeth. His body had been bound in webs just like hers, but only to his waist. Below that, his legs had been meticulously stripped to the bone. Only a few dark tendons and ligaments hung from his knees and ankles.

The creature was slowly consuming him, limb by limb.

While he was still alive.

Not for much longer . . .

Megan used all her resolve to avoid looking horrified as she scanned back up his body. Vargas was right: the thing had taken them for food. She glanced around the burrow for any other survivors: DeLuca, the Johnson family, Emma.

It was too dark, and her sight still too poor, to see much beyond Rizzo.

Any moment now, the arachnid would return and likely feast on him before her eyes—a gruesome preview to her own eventual fate.

Her vision cleared a little more. The arachnid stood over another cocooned body.

The head and shoulders had been cleanly stripped of all their flesh and muscle, making the face unrecognizable. Megan looked down at the lower half of the body, fearing the worst. Emma's hiking pants and boots confirmed it.

The arachnid sank its fangs into Emma's upper body, systematically cutting straight lines across her chest, going lower each time. Ripping off chunks of flesh and swallowing. In less than a minute, it had opened her rib cage and torn out a lung to gorge upon.

Megan had never felt more horrified in her life.

"Megan, please tell me . . ." Rizzo croaked. "Is my Emma safe?"

Megan realized that the pastor could not see the horrors happening right behind him. With everyone's impending death a certainty, it served no purpose to inform the pastor that his daughter was already dead and being consumed by this nightmarish creature.

"She's safe, Pastor," Megan said, fighting back tears. "Emma escaped with Ryan a while ago."

"Thank God," Rizzo mumbled, drooling blood.

But she knew that no one was getting out of here alive. The fate of DeLuca and the Johnsons was now chillingly clear. Even though she couldn't see them, their bodies were around here somewhere.

Likely in various states of consumption too . . .

Soon, the monster would be tearing the lungs out of her lifeless body as well.

Rizzo swallowed hard. "Please, if you make it out of here, tell Emma how much I love her."

Megan nodded. "I promise, Pastor. I promise."

Rizzo tried to smile, but his mouth quickly straightened. He took a final, bubbling breath, and his body relaxed, his suffering finally at an end.

She briefly closed her eyes and prayed this would all go away.

The sounds of tearing flesh sent a chill down her spine.

She hoped the end would be fast.

Megan half opened her eyes and glanced across to the arachnid, not daring to attract its attention.

It continued digging inside Emma's ribcage, making fast work of her liver.

Then it sprang up and darted toward the distant, dimly lit burrow entrance. A heartbeat later, it scuttled away, no doubt alerted to other prey.

She expected it back soon to finish off the Rizzo family.

Then it would be her turn.

CHAPTER
THIRTY-TWO

What the hell are you doing, Ricky?

Vargas stood beside the burrow entrance, his back planted against the mountain's rocky face. It took a lot to piss him off, but he was now firmly in that territory, to the point where his anger had overridden his fear.

He was angry at himself for choosing this moment to be brave. Furious at his life for bringing him to this sorry pass.

But most of all, he was angry at that god-awful creature for picking them off one by one so easily and for acting as if it were invincible.

No one's invincible, asshole.

He dropped the heavy tree limb that he had just swung against the arachnid's thick cable of webs. Maybe this would confuse the hell out of the damned thing, though he had no clue. He hoped to send a signal that webs had been disturbed in every part of the forest, and get that creature out of its nest long enough to rescue Megan.

He craned his neck around the mouth of the burrow and shined Megan's UV flashlight inside. The tunnel was wider than he had expected—maybe eight feet. The blue cable ran deep, like a huge glow stick in a storm drain. But so far, the monster had not emerged.

Vargas wrestled on Ryan's backpack, which he had salvaged from the riverbank. The damp fabric and straps cooled his back and shoulders. He picked up the pitchfork, determined to give the next few minutes everything he had.

Still, no sound came from the burrow.

How much encouragement did this damned thing need?

Vargas edged inside the tunnel and took a few steps. He kept close to the fractured, damp wall while angling the UV beam down the shallow incline, listening for the faintest sound of the arachnid heading his way.

Each step forward seemed like a slow descent into hell. He winced as his boots crunched against loose gravel. He held the pitchfork forward in his right hand, like a lance.

The air was humid and much warmer than outside.

Sweat trickled down his temples.

Something flitted silently past him, brushing his cheek.

With an inward gasp, Vargas dropped to one knee. He swept the UV beam across the ceiling as a bat burst out of the tunnel's mouth.

Then something rustled deeper inside the cave. Vargas turned the UV light quickly, and its muted glow revealed the arachnid's shell.

Vargas flattened against the cave wall and switched off the flashlight. He stayed deathly still, praying that the thing hadn't detected him.

His survival depended on Megan's theories. If the thing couldn't see him or smell him, all he had to do was not hit a web.

Right?

A soft clattering approached.

Vargas tensed. The creature was heading right toward him.

"Fuck me," he breathed.

The clatter of eight galloping legs grew louder as it thundered up the tunnel. It would reach him in seconds.

Vargas discounted the idea of ramming the fork into the creature's side. He had learned to pick his fights carefully. If the spider went searching the forest, that would give anyone left alive a chance to escape.

A close-quarters fight would be the last resort.

And it could happen right now.

The web cable still had a slight residual glow from where he had earlier shined the UV rays. Vargas dared a glance.

The arachnid powered up the incline, legs on either side of the cable, body brushing it—perhaps to monitor any more disturbances.

Vargas tried to stop his body from shaking as he pressed against the cave wall, trying to be as flat as possible.

The arachnid raced right past him without slowing, inches from his chest, and left its stench hanging in the close air. It then burst out of the burrow entrance and disappeared into the dark forest, in search of its prey.

"Later, motherfucker!" Vargas yelled out, amazed that his ruse had worked.

After waiting for a minute, he activated the UV light and pressed deeper. He could move faster now, confident he wasn't running straight into two sharp fangs.

The tunnel leveled off, and his beam shot into a wide-open space twenty yards ahead.

He advanced, conscious that the arachnid could return at any minute. Scared of what he might find, yet committed to seeing this through, whatever the outcome.

A coppery stench hit him, and he felt queasy at the thought of its source.

Vargas reached the end of the tunnel and swept the UV beam around a cavern the size of a cathedral. Glimmers of moonlight punched through the roof in several areas. The sound of water dripping into a pool echoed around the walls. At the back of the burrow stood a pile of bones thirty feet high. Thousands of them—a mix of animal and human. The bones near the bottom were darker in shade than those on top. The entire cave smelled of putrefaction and decay.

Vargas lowered the beam to where the thick cable of web led to a bed of dry moss. Maybe the point where the arachnid sat waiting for a signal from the forest.

"Pretty shitty crib you got here, asshole!" he called out into the darkness.

He moved the UV beam away from the cable, cutting it over the ground.

The sight made him shake his head in disbelief.

A spiral of skeletons led out from the bed of moss. Arranged in tight coils that reached farther with each revolution until they fanned all the way out to the distant walls.

He guessed there had to be several thousand. Like the bone

midden, this formation also appeared to have a certain order. The remains closest to the bed of moss looked ancient—hundreds of years old, at least. Dried and cracked with age. Some animals, Vargas couldn't even recognize. Each skeleton had a few bright-blue threads around the skull, ribs, and legs.

Newer victims were near the outer reaches, like the youngest growth rings of a tree. That was where he would likely find the victims from the church group.

"Can anyone hear me?" he called out. "Megan?"

A faint murmur came from a dark alcove to his left. A survivor? Or was it just the wind coming through a fissure in the ceiling?

Vargas headed toward it, stepping carefully over the arcs of human and animal bones, and avoiding the webs at all costs.

"Yo," he said. "It's Ricky. Anyone there?"

A voice mumbled in the darkness.

A woman.

Perhaps he could rescue at least one of the captives. Optimism rose inside him, though not enough to quell his terror of the monster that could come clambering back into its home at any moment.

He trained his beam on the last row of skeletons and crept closer. The first thing he noticed was a dead deer that had not yet been stripped bare. Perhaps the one he saw getting ripped into the canopy yesterday. The only thing left was its head, with one black eye staring vacantly upward.

Vargas moved his beam to the next body of bones. He gasped at the sight.

DeLuca's head, arms, and legs were still intact, but his torso had been devoured. The shredded clothes, bunched next to his shoulder blade, confirmed it was him.

Vargas had seen some messed-up things in his life. People beaten and maimed. He'd seen his share of dead bodies too.

But this was something on a different scale altogether.

Just keep going, Ricky.

Vargas moved the UV beam slowly to the left. The blue light revealed the bodies of the Johnsons and their grandkid.

The grandparents' bodies were straitjacketed in hundreds of webs. Jim had puncture wounds in his throat and appeared to have bled out. The creature had eaten Maryann's arms. Connor had been completely consumed and was recognizable only by the size of his skeleton.

Vargas fought back the urge to vomit. The nauseating stench did not help.

"Ricky?" someone moaned.

Vargas spun to his left and shined his light over two rigid corpses in half-eaten states. Then, farther . . .

It was Megan. Still alive, cocooned in webs.

It didn't take a rocket scientist to work out who the two corpses were next to her, but Vargas couldn't bring himself to look at Emma's body.

Megan squinted. "Is that you?"

She sounded weak. But he had a chance to save her from an end beyond anyone's wildest nightmares.

"It's me."

She cracked a pained smile. "I knew you'd come."

"Yeah, right," he said while rifling through Ryan's backpack. "You caught me on a good day."

"Thank you," Megan said tenderly.

"Okay, let's get you outta these webs."

Vargas fished out a hunting knife and whipped off the sheath.

He planted the serrated edge over the webs binding Megan's knees. Then he sawed back and forth, carving through a bundle of webs at a time.

Within a minute, he'd managed to free Megan up to her stomach. Halfway done.

He worked the knife efficiently, not wasting a second, putting as much force into it as he safely could. Megan stayed silent, letting him concentrate on his work.

His forearm ached as he cut away the final few inches from around her chest. Sweat dripped from his brow. Finally, he had cut through the cocoon and pulled it apart from her body.

Vargas grabbed Megan's arms and hauled her to a sitting position.

"Thank you," she said groggily.

"Can you move?"

"I'll try. What about the rest? Is anyone else . . ."

His somber look told her all she needed to know. She returned his grim acknowledgment.

He helped her to her feet. She leaned against him—unsteady on her legs, but that would do.

Vargas turned Megan toward the tunnel. "Let's go."

"What's the plan?"

"The plan is to get the fuck outta here."

Before he could take a step forward, a scuttling sound echoed down the tunnel, growing louder by the second.

The creature was coming back.

CHAPTER

THIRTY-THREE

Vargas knew that he had only moments to come up with something if he didn't want them both to end up in the beast's belly. It was debatable whether Megan could even make it out of the burrow on her own, never mind face down an angry creature that had just learned of an uninvited guest.

An animal screech resonated up the tunnel, followed by sounds of a frantic struggle. Perhaps a bear, putting up a last-ditch effort against the arachnid. Its struggling would prove futile, but it might give Vargas a little more time before the monster reached them.

Finally, a plan formed in his mind. A long shot, but better than no shot at all. Vargas passed Megan the UV flashlight. He knelt by Ryan's pack and reached inside.

"The gunpowder . . ." Megan murmured. She looked ready to collapse under her own weight.

"The motherfuckin' gunpowder!" Vargas replied. "It's the only shot we got. We burn his little bachelor pad to the ground and hope it distracts him long enough for us to sneak outta here."

He grabbed the small powder keg out of the backpack and set it on the ground.

Vargas squeezed the hunting knife between two of the lid's oaken slats, rapidly working a gap. The tip of the blade punctured through what looked like wax paper.

"Shine it down here," he said.

Megan tottered toward him with the UV light.

"Yeah baby," he shouted.

Inside the paper covering, he could see black, granular powder. And it still appeared dry.

"Not bad for two-hundred-year-old gunpowder. That is, if it still burns."

And that was a big *if*. For all he knew, it might fizzle out with a hiss, just as their lives would shortly thereafter. He had no way of telling, but he had to try. Vargas angled the keg down until the gunpowder streamed out like sand through an hourglass.

"Try not to blow us up too," Megan said.

"No promises," he replied, smiling.

The sounds of the struggle up the tunnel ended abruptly. Clearly, whatever animal was fighting for its life had just lost. It brought an eerie silence to the burrow.

"Keep me lit up," he said to Megan, nodding at the flashlight.

She shined it on the area around his boots, and he moved off, laying a trail of gunpowder in a wide arc across the spiral of skeletons.

"Careful of those webs," Megan whispered.

But there was no avoiding the ones spread across the ground in the cave. It wouldn't matter much longer, anyway.

In a few moments, the creature would have bigger problems than losing its dinner.

He continued forty yards across the dark center of the arachnid's lair, listening intently while laying down a constant trail of powder.

The keg grew lighter in his hands, and the stream of powder thinned to a trickle. The keg was nearly empty.

Would this be enough?

Vargas remembered a second powder keg, but it had been in Emma's backpack as the thing dragged her down here. It had to be here somewhere.

He would just have to face seeing her dead body.

His gut clenched. He had to sprint back while he still had time. But as he turned, the UV light cut away from him and toward the tunnel entrance, plunging him into darkness.

"What the hell?" he shouted.

Across the cave, Megan held the beam squarely on the arachnid. It stood close to its bed of moss, with a deer in its fangs.

As if sensing their presence, the creature immediately dropped the limp carcass. It hit the ground like a sack of potatoes.

Vargas stood paralyzed for a split second.

Come on, Ricky!

He patted his pockets for the Zippo.

Empty.

He had put everything in Ryan's backpack earlier.

Suddenly, the creature let out an ear-shattering hiss. Vargas clutched his ears and tried to ignore the stabbing pain in his head.

"Megan!" he bellowed. "Grab the lighter! Ryan's side pouch!"

It was no use. Megan couldn't hear him over the creature's screeching. He could see her dark figure across the lair, clutching her ears in pain.

The arachnid raised its head, revealing its razor-edged fangs, and burst across the boneyard, directly toward Vargas.

Vargas turned and ran toward the back of the burrow, away from Megan so the creature couldn't easily take them both down. She tried to help with the UV light, but he was moving too fast. His boots crunched down on brittle bones as he sprinted, trying to draw the monster closer to the gunpowder.

Vargas reached the mound of bones.

Let's see you climb this, asshole . . .

He started up, and his boot clattered against a grinning deer skull. His right forearm pushed off from a rib cage, snapping bones. The shattered edges scraped his flesh.

The chattering noise from the arachnid neared.

He reached up and grabbed several bones. They fell around him in a mini avalanche that piled below his feet. It created a sound like a lunatic's xylophone as he scrambled to get a solid hold on *anything*. Eventually, he found a long bone that was stuck in place. Vargas grabbed it with both hands and dragged himself a few feet higher.

He glanced back, though it was too dark to see anything beyond the UV beam focusing on him.

"Ricky, watch out!"

Vargas tensed. At any moment, he expected to feel those fangs in the back of his neck. He clutched what looked like a thigh bone, and yanked it free from the mound. Then he turned for a battle that he fully expected to lose.

Regardless, he would make the creature pay dearly.

* * *

Megan had to use every bit of strength just to keep the flashlight raised. Every limb seemed to lack the basic strength to function. Only adrenaline kept her standing—that and the thought of the arachnid pulling her ribs apart and gorging on her insides.

Although at the moment, Vargas seemed much closer to losing his life. Megan watched him climb several feet up the pile of remains. A bone in his left hand, primed to attack. The arachnid stood below, front legs upraised like a tarantula about to strike. Maybe the posture was to show its dominance. If so, it needn't have bothered.

Megan tried to step forward. Her thighs cramped, and she winced in pain. Whatever sedative the creature had injected her with was clearly designed to keep its prey in a weakened state.

She had to shake this off.

Across the cavern, Vargas looked in her direction and tried to shout something. But the creature's piercing hiss made the words inaudible.

I can't do a goddamn thing. Not strong enough, and he's too far away. And do I even have the guts?

The arachnid sprang upward toward Vargas.

"Ricky, watch out!" Megan screamed.

He lurched to the side and swung the bone against the spider's head. It clattered off the upper shell and snapped in his hand.

Vargas tried to scramble to his left. But the arachnid antici-pated the move and lunged at his legs. Both fangs sank deep into his left calf. He screamed out in agony.

"NO!" Megan cried out, her voice strong for the first time since her capture.

She flexed her arms and legs. Feeling and strength were

quickly returning. She grabbed the pocketknife from her pants and flicked open the blade.

As she stepped forward, fear overwhelmed her, and she froze. She could barely watch. She wanted to run like hell, but something inside told her to stop.

Vargas writhed. She couldn't hear his scream, but she could see it. Mouth wide open. Bulging eyes. He flailed desperately about with his hands, searching for another loose bone—searching for anything to fight off the predator.

The arachnid shook its head violently to the side, launching Vargas off the mountain of bones. He hurtled through dim moonlight and landed hard against the cave floor a dozen feet away.

Vargas skidded through the bones that the creature had spread around the burrow, arms protectively covering his head. He slid to a stop near the center of the vast space.

This time, she heard his agonized roar.

"RICKY!" Megan shouted, taking two steps toward him.

The arachnid scuttled down from the bone pile and moved in slowly for the kill. Almost as if it was enjoying the moment. Toying with him. Taking its time to end the life that had the audacity to enter its home.

Megan cast the light on Vargas, hoping he had something planned. Her foggy mind couldn't come up with anything beyond the assessment that they were screwed.

Vargas raised his head. One eye was swollen shut, and blood dripped from his lower lip. He lifted his shaking right hand and jerked his thumb up and down. Then he rolled onto his back to face the arachnid.

The lighter!

Megan remembered Vargas putting all his belongings into

Ryan's backpack earlier. She grabbed the pack and tipped out the contents of the main compartment. Just camping equipment. Where the hell was it?

She zipped open the side pockets and threw out a compass, a New York Islanders cap, and, last of all, a Zippo lighter.

She turned, fearing the worst.

The arachnid had neared to within pouncing distance of Vargas. The closer it got, the softer its hiss became.

"Light the goddamn place up!" Vargas yelled.

"But it might kill you!" she cried back.

"MEGAN, DO IT!"

She knew that this was probably her last chance. *Their* last chance. And her next move might well end Vargas before the thing could finish him off.

Go for it, she said to herself. *Don't stall; don't debate. Do it!*

She flipped open the lid and thumbed the flint wheel. Sparks brightened the immediate area, soon replaced by a low orange glow from the flame.

The arachnid scuttled toward Vargas. Moving in for the kill now that it had taken away the chance of an escape.

Megan tossed the Zippo onto the gunpowder and staggered backward.

She held her breath, praying . . .

Suddenly, sparks erupted from the ground as the combustible trail ignited.

Crackling fire rushed around the burrow in a wide arc, racing directly for Vargas and the arachnid. The blazing gunpowder brightened the entirety of the underground lair. Throughout the cave, thousands of webs burst into flames, as if someone had sprayed them with an accelerant.

The arachnid screeched in rage as fire raced through the cavern. The powder trail behind Vargas ignited, cutting him off from Megan. Cutting him off from the only way out.

On one side of the fire stood Vargas and the creature. On the other side, Megan and the exit.

The gunpowder ignited every filament of web around it. A giant wall of flames swelled upward, driving both Ricky and Megan back in opposite directions.

Megan scrambled away from the scorching fire, instinctively clutching the scar on her arm—an indelible memento from the state fair.

The moment that took everything away from me . . .

On the other side of the fire, Vargas got unsteadily to his feet, staggering away from the creature and the overwhelming heat.

"Megan, GO!" he bellowed. "Get the hell out of here while one of us has a chance!"

"I'm not leaving you, Ricky!"

"For fuck's sake, go! NOW!"

Megan spun toward the exit of the tunnel. It was now or never. And the flames were too high for her to try to save him. She had no choice but to leave.

But I can't live with myself if I run . . . And I might not live if I don't . . .

She rubbed the scar on her arm and turned back toward the fire with a newfound determination. Back toward Ricky Vargas.

This time will be different, she promised herself.

But just as last time, she froze. Her body wouldn't let her move.

CHAPTER

THIRTY-FOUR

Flames seared Vargas's back. Fire, fed by an uncountable number of combustible webs, cut off any chance of an escape to his left or right, engulfing him in a horseshoe of death. He shuffled forward a few inches on one knee, trying to avoid getting burned alive. His other leg was splayed to the side, the calf dripping with blood where the creature's fangs had stabbed him.

He hissed out a pained breath through clenched teeth. The fangs had punched through his muscle, right to the bone, though he felt none of the weakness that Megan was visibly experiencing. He must have kicked free before the monster injected him with its venom, or maybe hitting the bone kept it from delivering the full dose.

But the agony of the wound and the stench of his singeing

hair were nothing compared to what he now faced: the ultimate challenge of his life.

The arachnid stood in front of him, blocking his route. Motionless, as if trying to sense what was happening in its lair as thousands of webs crackled and burned. The flames glinted off its glossy black shell. Two steps forward would bring the fangs into biting range once again. That was probably the spider's next move.

The wall of fire narrowed Vargas's possible escape routes to one. He had no choice but to fight the creature head-on, hoping the overstimulation of the inferno around them would dull the spider's senses enough that he might wound it.

Vargas searched the immediate area for any sharp bones. A few lay close to the arachnid's legs.

Too risky.

Think, Ricky, you son of a bitch. You always get out of tight spots.

The creature hunched down on its eight legs. Its mouth twitched repeatedly, letting out a creepy chattering sound.

Was it preparing to pounce, or suffering from the overwhelming heat?

Vargas glanced over his shoulder to where Megan had stood. He raised his arm to shield his face from the blazing fire.

He could no longer see her.

She must have run . . . *Good.*

He couldn't blame her. After all, he had insisted that she run. How far she would actually get in her present condition was anyone's guess. Her escape might only delay the inevitable, now that his plan had tanked harder than the New York Jets did almost every season.

He turned back to face the arachnid.

The beady black eyes seemed to stare at him, while its enormous fangs dripped with something that wasn't blood.

This motherfucker can't see for shit . . . Right?

He bowed his head for a moment. It wasn't supposed to end like this. Yesterday, he had thought that after this trip he'd be flush with cash and banging college chicks on summer break in Ocean City.

Why the hell did I choose now to grow a conscience?

* * *

Megan shook off her indecision. She had only moments to act. Ignoring Emma's exposed skeletal remains, she crouched beside her blood-drenched backpack and yanked it open. Dug her hand inside and pulled out the contents. A compressed sleeping bag. Dried food. Clothes. The second keg of black powder. And at the bottom, a blue blanket.

She shook it out to its full length.

Big enough for the job.

Megan wrapped the blanket around her head, shoulders, and body, leaving a narrow opening to see through. Then she headed toward the wall of fire in the middle of the burrow.

The flames now illuminated the full vastness of the cavernous lair. The only way to save Vargas was to head through the fire. She could barely make him out through the flames. He was crouching on one knee, facing the arachnid, which had not yet attacked. But that could change any second as the creature, not understanding the destruction ripping through its home, began to fight anything and everything around it.

As she neared the edge of the flames, visions of Mike and

Ethan, trapped in their swing chair, flashed in her mind. Her hesitating out of fear. The horrific consequences of backing away.

History would not repeat itself today. Nothing would bring back her husband and son, but if she could just save Vargas and herself . . .

Better to die trying than live with backing down a second time.

Her boots kicked bones as she strode directly toward Vargas.

The heat was getting unbearable, and the flames showed no sign of weakening. The vast network of webs burned like confetti soaked in kerosene.

Megan took a deep breath and shouted over the cacophony of crackling and burning. "Ricky!"

He remained motionless on the other side of the fire, staring at the creature. It inched backward and forward, as if confused.

Megan broke into a sprint, looking down to make sure nothing tripped her.

At any moment, she expected the blanket to burst into flames. But it was too late to stop.

Heat engulfed her as the arachnid's hissing filled her ears.

She took three long leaps, powering through the flames before they could take her down. In the blink of an eye, she reached the other side and skidded to a stop next to Vargas. He still faced the creature, as if lost in thought or stunned by the sheer strangeness of events.

Megan grabbed his shoulder. "Ricky!"

He didn't flinch.

"Vargas!" she shouted close to his ear.

His head snapped in her direction. "How the hell did you . . ."

She stooped by his side and hooked her arm around his chest. "On your feet. We're leaving."

"My leg is fucked. You should have gone."

"If we don't go now, we're both fucked. Now move!"

Vargas nodded. "You got it, boss."

He grimaced as she helped him to his feet. Both turned to look at the arachnid. Still within striking distance, it now seemed oblivious to their presence. It snapped its fangs repeatedly at the flames and falling debris, as if unable to lock onto its prey.

Megan wrapped the singed blanket around both her and Vargas's head and shoulders and turned back toward the fire. He hopped around until they faced the tunnel entrance.

"Just run like hell!" she commanded.

The arachnid let out a high-pitched scream that resonated through her body.

It knows we're here . . .

Vargas glanced across to her. His wide-eyed expression required no interpretation. They ducked and ran through the fire, clinging to each other until they reached the other side.

Their blanket shroud was now engulfed in flames. Megan shook it off them and quickly patted out the fire that had caught on Vargas's pants.

Vargas collapsed to his knees in pain. "You go ahead," he breathed.

"No chance. We do this together."

"Jeez, I'd hate to work for you."

"Luckily, that'll never happen."

Megan hoisted Vargas to his feet again. If the creature had, in fact, homed in on them, they had only moments to escape. Snatching up Emma's backpack, she helped Vargas limp up the tunnel toward the exit as smoke billowed all around them. They brushed against the thick cable of webs that ran out of the cave into the forest, but at this point they had no time to be delicate.

The cave's mouth was maybe fifty yards ahead. Forty yards . . .
Thirty.

For a moment, Megan entertained the hope that they might
escape this nightmare alive. That hope shattered as the arachnid's
piercing scream split the air. It sounded right behind them.

Megan spun to face the back of the burrow, praying that the
creature hadn't managed to follow them.

"Oh shit," Vargas said.

The arachnid burst through the flames, completely ablaze. Its
legs flailed wildly as its fangs snapped, trying to rip apart any
sentient thing, to destroy the source of its pain. It crushed bones
under its weight as it raced up the tunnel.

The creature was manic. Desperate. Angry.

And it was heading directly for them.

CHAPTER

THIRTY-FIVE

Megan gripped Vargas's T-shirt and hauled him forward. Only twenty yards to go. Behind them, the screeching and the gnashing of fangs closed in.

Just how close, she dare not guess. A second wasted turning around to check might well be her last.

Her lungs screamed for fresh air as she wheezed in smoke between repeated coughs. Every step up the incline felt like pulling a coal barge upstream. If, by some miracle, they pulled through this, it was a horror she'd never forget.

Vargas struggled mightily to keep up, panting, hopping uphill beside her, and groaning whenever the injured leg bumped something.

A few more steps, and they would burst out of the cave and into open woods. But she could feel the presence of what was coming after them. Megan finally darted a glance over her shoulder.

The arachnid sounded like a freight train roaring up the tunnel.

The thick cable of webs had erupted from a flickering blue glow into a fireball, racing alongside the monster to the cave's exit. Either one meant death to the two frail humans.

Vargas was slowing down, exhausted. At this pace, the creature would overtake them before they got outside. They had to do something right now.

Then the realization hit Megan.

If this monster escapes, it's going to keep killing.

Again . . . and again . . . and again.

She stopped running and let go of Vargas. He turned back to face her, looking surprised. "What the hell are you doing!"

"This ends here, Ricky," Megan replied. "Keep going. I'm right behind you."

"Are you *crazy?*" he shouted back.

"Ricky, GO!" she said, pushing him forward.

Before he had a chance to reply, Megan dropped Emma's backpack by her feet, reached down, and lifted out the powder keg.

The arachnid was nearly on her, screaming in agonized fury. Fire, fed by the webs, raced behind it, toward the exit.

She slipped the pocketknife out of her pants and stabbed through the keg's lid.

"Megan!" Vargas yelled from the mouth of the tunnel. "For fuck's sake, RUN!"

Flames engulfed the shrieking creature. Enraged, it came at Megan, fangs ripping at the air.

She lifted the keg above her right shoulder and took a deep, shaking breath.

Wait for it . . .

The burning creature locked in on Megan and crouched to spring.

Now!

"Burn in hell, you son of a bitch!"

She heaved the powder keg with both arms. It arced through the air, turning end over end, and crashed into the snapping fangs of the monster. The fangs easily splintered the wood, covering the creature's mouth with black powder.

Megan spun and sprinted for the cave entrance.

"GET DOWN!" she shouted at Vargas.

Vargas dived to the left of the entrance and she lunged to the right, wrapping her arms around her head and curling into a fetal position.

A moment later, a booming explosion ripped through the air.

The ground shuddered, and small pebbles pattered down around Megan.

A fireball billowed out of the cave and into the tinder-dry forest. Shards of the arachnid's shell and bloody chunks of sinew shot out of the cave and splat down on the riverbank.

Megan turned onto her back and screamed with primal joy

Vargas screamed right alongside her.

"That's what I'm fucking talking about!" he crowed.

But the sense of relief vanished in the next instant. The flames raced along the thousands of webs into the thick forest, igniting the dry groundcover and crawling up tree bark.

"Oh shit," Megan gasped. She scrambled across to Vargas, who stared in shock at the building conflagration.

A thousand lines of fire exploded from one tree to the next, racing into the distance. Within a minute, the woods all around them had caught fire. The all-but-invisible webs revealed themselves in their own destruction.

The pace of the spreading blaze was breathtaking. Strands of fire rocketed down the incline in the direction of the bus. They shot up the trail toward the cabin. In the distance, the fire disappeared over the brow of a hill, then reappeared moments later, racing up the side of a distant mountain, illuminating the vastness of the creature's territory.

Everywhere she looked, the bone-dry forest burned. Branches burst into flames, and treetops went up like struck matches.

In the time it took them to recognize their situation, a forest fire was closing in on them from all sides. If they stayed a minute longer, they would surely burn to death.

They had just escaped hell, only to find themselves right back in it.

Even the foaming Class V rapids seemed to be ablaze with reflected fire. Across the river, flames hopped from treetop to treetop up the side of the mountain.

She pulled Vargas to his feet and turned toward the river.

"No, no, no," he said. "You're not seriously thinking we . . ."

Her silence was his answer.

CHAPTER THIRTY-SIX

"There's no other way," Megan said, though she harbored no illusions. Jumping into this maelstrom was likely just death by other means. And the only thing she remembered about white-water rafting was the five-minute tutorial she got years ago before rafting with her husband in New Zealand.

That was on a big, self-bailing inflatable boat, with paddles and life vests for everyone.

But even drowning beat the torture waiting if they stayed on the riverbank any longer. Just about everything beat getting burned alive.

Burned alive . . .

The roar and the blistering heat all around them overwhelmed Megan's senses. They had to jump. Now.

Vargas stared at her. Beyond him, on the opposite side of the rapids, the fires blazed higher and higher. A wall of flames, brightening the night sky with an orange hue. Hundreds, maybe thousands of acres were being destroyed.

"So," Vargas said. "We just dive in and hope for the best?"

"At least that way we'll have a chance."

After escaping the monster's clutches, to die in the river seemed a cruel irony.

He gazed down at the water. The river had already taken Ryan's life. Maybe it was about to take theirs.

"Try and stay near the middle of the rapids to avoid falling trees and debris," she said. "When we reach the bus downriver, swim for shore. And keep your feet out in front of you—they're your bumpers."

"Got it," Vargas replied. "And when I break both my legs in the first minute, what do I do then?"

"Try and keep both broken legs in front of you."

Her wiseass comment got a smirk from him.

"Say, don't suppose you have a pool noodle handy in that backpack."

She smiled and moved to Vargas's side. The heat was almost unbearable as flames consumed the entire forest.

A loud crack echoed from above.

They both whipped their heads upward.

An enormous sycamore, entirely on fire, was about to topple into the river, onto the very rock they were standing on.

"RICKY!" Megan shouted. "JUMP NOW!"

She grabbed his hand, and the two leaped into the roaring rapids, just as the flaming sycamore came crashing down onto the rock.

Instantly, they were whisked fifty yards downstream.

Megan kicked her legs and pulled with both arms, trying

to get her head above the foam. Her boot hit a rock. Her arm scraped something, instantly drawing blood. Eventually, the dark sky appeared above her, and she sucked in a deep breath.

Vargas rose by her side and coughed.

"Get your legs up!" she yelled.

"Trying," he gasped.

Seconds later, his boots jutted above the surface. He let out an anguished cry—must have bumped the injured leg. As they steered with their arms and tried to look downstream, the rapids tossed them about like rag dolls. Megan's thigh slammed hard against a rock. She opened her mouth to cry out, only to be dragged back down beneath the surface.

Chilly water rushed down her throat.

Vargas grabbed her, pulling her closer, and she got her head up.

Megan spat, then drew in a breath.

They were traveling fast down the roaring river, past burning forest on both sides.

A log slammed into Vargas's back, knocking the wind out of him. He gasped for breath, trying to hang on to Megan.

He dipped under the swell, clutching her arm, and emerged a moment later, taking rapid, shallow breaths and staring at the smoke-filled sky.

Megan's body shook from the cold. The rapids seemed even faster here.

"We're speeding up!" Vargas cried out.

Then Megan remembered. *The waterfall . . .*

Just above where they parked the bus two days ago, they had seen that lovely, scenic waterfall.

Just ahead, both banks were free of flames. And the river disappeared from view. This led to the ominous conclusion.

"Waterfall!" Megan cried out. "Try and make it to shore!"

The current pulled Vargas under for a moment, and he slammed into a rock, bruising—perhaps breaking—some ribs. He popped back to the surface and looked ahead. Now maybe he understood what Megan was shouting about.

They both swam furiously for the river's edge, using the last of their strength to fight the rushing current. But the force of the water twisted and turned their bodies, making it nearly impossible to fight.

The falls were less than thirty yards away.

Twenty . . .

The river pulled them away from each other. Vargas's head disappeared again.

"Ricky!"

She couldn't reach him, so she pulled for shore with everything she had.

Ten yards away.

Any kind of rescue attempt was impossible. Vargas was on his own.

The last few strokes took everything out of her, and her limbs finally refused to obey.

A moment later, she felt the riverbed fall out from beneath her, and she hurtled over the edge, arms and legs flailing.

Her body plummeted a dozen feet before crashing into the foaming river below. The current twisted and tumbled her underwater, holding her down with the mass of water coming from above.

She was trapped, unable to break out of the vortex and knowing that if she didn't, she was moments from drowning.

Something whacked her—a tree limb that had followed her over the falls and got caught in the same deadly spin cycle. The momentum pushed her out of the whirlpool and spat her into calmer waters ahead.

She sucked in the life-giving air.

She was alive.

But Ricky . . .

Megan swam diagonally to a gentle eddy at the water's edge, and her knees eventually crunched onto gravel. She scrambled to dry land and collapsed onto all fours, gasping for breath. Even soaked and dripping, she could still feel the heat from the fast-spreading forest fire. She had cuts and scrapes all over her arms and legs.

The backpack had protected her somewhat from rocks and debris. Megan shucked it off and flopped down on the shore. She searched the water. Still nothing.

Come on, Ricky, you can do it. Please . . .

As if in answer, Vargas's body jettisoned from the tumult below the waterfall, close to the bank. He drew in a deep, braying breath. He was alive.

He floundered over to Megan and up onto shore, clutching his ribs.

"You bastard," she gasped. "You had me worried."

He slumped down by her side. "Nothing to worry about. My ribs broke the fall."

She burst out laughing and wrapped her arms around him in joy.

"Don't squeeze and don't make me laugh!" he said with a tired smile.

Megan couldn't believe it. For the first time in two days, they weren't in immediate, mortal danger. A huge burden had been lifted off her. The release was immense. She felt like a shaken-up bottle of soda that had just been opened.

The two of them lay in silence for the next few moments, catching their breath. They needed to get to a hospital, but they were alive.

Megan turned and took in the view. The entire forest was burning, but they were safe here, on the bank of the river, in a large clearing. A few hundred yards behind them was the road where they had parked the bus. The flames had consumed the entire vehicle, gutting it with everything inside.

"Ricky," Megan said. "The bus . . ."

Vargas turned and looked at the terrible sight.

"For fuck's sake," he replied, shaking his head in disbelief. "Well, it's not every day you lose half a million dollars."

"What are you gonna do?"

Vargas looked lost in thought for a moment.

"Well," he said, "I can't ever go back to New York or I'm a dead man. Something tells me the people those drugs belong to won't buy my story."

Megan took in the gravity of his situation.

In the distance, the beat of search-and-rescue helicopters grew louder, as did the approaching sirens.

"Thank you for coming back to save me," Megan finally said, resting her head on his shoulder.

He leaned his head on hers. "And thanks for saving me, boss."

CHAPTER
THIRTY-
SEVEN

Megan sat in Cumberland Hospital's waiting room, surrounded by several people who had managed to escape the inferno. Everyone exchanged sorrowful glances. Some had bandaged wounds, blackened faces, torn clothing. A few fired off texts and browsed the net on their phones, looking at the latest news.

She was willing to bet that none of them knew the actual cause of the fire.

Did we get anyone killed? Did we really cause all this?

She quickly dismissed the thought. This was all the arachnid's fault. It alone caused this destruction. Still, seeing campers from far away being rushed into the ER disturbed her.

Megan had already seen the triage nurse. Only scrapes and bruises, but they wanted to keep her overnight for observation. But coming to terms with all that had happened would have to wait for another day. She heaved a deep sigh and stared at some of the posters on the wall.

It was hard to focus on the words. Now that the scientifically inexplicable threat had vanished and the adrenaline had abated, the only thing keeping her eyes open was the train of mental images from the past two days. Crazy chases. Gruesome scenes. Horror that was once beyond her imagination.

The creature.

"Jesus Christ," she murmured.

Visions from inside the cave would stay with her for the rest of her life, joining the horror show of the state fair. The only consolation was that she and Vargas were alive.

Megan bowed her head at the thought of Pastor Rizzo and Emma, the Johnsons, DeLuca, and Ryan. All had met a horrible end. Maybe it was survivor's guilt taking over, but she questioned why she had been allowed to live and tell the tale.

If she should ever feel like telling it. Who would even believe her?

A set of double doors opened, and a nurse stood in the corridor with his hands on a wheelchair. In it sat Vargas, dressed in a light-green surgical gown, pulling an EKG machine alongside him. They had stitched up his leg, patched his ribs, and cleaned him up.

They broke into a wide grin at the same time.

Megan took comfort from his presence, and he seemed to do the same. Circumstances had brought together two people who appeared to have nothing in common. They had similarities that no one would have guessed based on appearances. And they had survived experiences they both would take to their graves.

"Don't suppose you grabbed me some smokes?" he asked Megan, smiling.

"Mr. Vargas," the nurse admonished.

"I'll take that as a no."

The nurse ignored him and looked to Megan. "Mrs. Forrester?"

"That's me."

The nurse scanned the ID bracelet on her wrist. "Now, Megan, if you'd please come this way. Since Ricky has requested your presence as his advocate and since your injuries are minor, you can stay in the same room for observation overnight."

Megan got up from the plastic chair, grabbed the backpack, and headed through the door.

The wheelchair's wheels squeaked on the polished floor as the nurse pushed Vargas forward. They entered a long ward with private rooms on either side. Most had their drapes drawn. A few doors stood ajar, with patients inside attached to monitoring equipment.

The distinctive smell of iodoform hung in the air, giving this place the typical hospital smell. Regardless, the air-conditioned environment was paradise compared to frigid white water or a burning forest.

A hiss broke the quiet. Megan's heart jumped, and her head whipped to the left.

A teenager lay in one of the rooms with a big bottle of soda in his hands. He was easing the cap open so it didn't spray all over.

"It's gonna be like this for a while," Vargas said.

Megan nodded as they continued through the ward.

So far, the rooms in the final third of the ward were empty. She had requested privacy if possible, though she wasn't expecting much, what with other patients bound to show up soon. The forest fire was still nowhere close to being under control.

The nurse wheeled Vargas inside a room with two single beds separated by a privacy curtain. The room was surprisingly well spaced, with a TV on the opposite wall. He helped Vargas out of the chair and into the bed, moving the EKG machine beside him.

"Is this really necessary?" Vargas protested. "I'm gonna live."

"And we're going to make sure of that," the nurse replied. He looked at the readouts for a moment, then pointed to a panel above the bedside cabinet. "Pull that cord in an emergency. Is there anything you both need?"

"You got any tequila?"

"I wish," the nurse replied. "Try and get some rest. You guys won't get disturbed down here. I'll make sure the other nurses give you some peace and quiet until the shift change at six a.m."

Megan breathed a sigh of relief. Being woken up every two hours to get her vital signs checked would have been a drag.

"Thank you," she replied.

The nurse left the room.

Megan placed Emma's backpack on the floor in the opposite corner of the room. It wasn't much, but maybe returning it to Emma's mother back in New York might give some solace in her grief. Megan could relate all too well to losing one's spouse and child at the same time.

She hobbled back to the bed and lay down. Her limbs felt heavy, and she gave a long, tired sigh as she stared at the ceiling.

Vargas grabbed the TV remote and hit the power button.

The overhead screen flashed to life. He flipped through the channels. All news stations were broadcasting footage of the immense forest fire raging in West Virginia, and the hundreds of firefighters struggling to contain the blaze.

"I'd rather not see it," Megan said.

"Me neither," Vargas said, turning off the television.

With a groan, he repositioned himself on the bed. She could tell he was still in pain, though he would never admit it.

"What you thinking about?" he asked.

"What we tell the police tomorrow," Megan replied. "And what we tell the families of everyone who died."

"We'll figure it out tomorrow. Together."

She was surprised by his reply.

"I thought you'd be disappearing soon."

"Oh, I will. After we do the right thing first."

She smiled fondly at him. Maybe this experience had changed Vargas. Instilled some personal responsibility that she suspected had always been in hiding.

Megan stifled a yawn. "I'm beat."

"I think I could sleep for a week," Vargas said. "But for now . . ." He checked the clock on the wall: just after eleven p.m. "I'll settle for seven hours."

He switched off the light, casting the room into near darkness except for the regular dim-blue flashes from the EKG machine he was connected to.

"See you in the morning, boss."

"Good night, Ricky."

Megan slipped off her pants and crawled under the warm sheets. The soft pillow felt like paradise. She closed her eyes and thanked God that they were alive. Her eyelids grew heavy.

***

Megan's eyelids flew open.

A quiet hissing filled the room. Faint, but familiar in a bone-chilling way.

It can't be. Not here.

Her eyes tracked the source of the sound to the corner of the room. Emma's backpack was on the floor, torn open from the inside.

She followed the sound upward to the ceiling in the corner . . . and gasped.

There, dozens of fist-sized arachnids waited, hissing, motionless. Tiny versions of the monster that had wreaked such carnage in the national forest.

Vargas's EKG machine flashed its blinking blue light, illuminating, for a fleeting moment, hundreds of cobwebs. They festooned the ceiling, the cabinets, the TV, the trays, the floors. The threads stretched across both their beds, crisscrossing less than an inch above their faces, arms, legs—surrounding them everywhere, attuned to detect the slightest vibration in the room.

All the webs led back to the ceiling in the corner, where the little creatures perched, motionless. Waiting. Hungry.

The EKG's light blinked off, and Megan was plunged into darkness again. Her breathing grew rapid and shallow as the fear overwhelmed her.

The light blinked back on. The webs were spun right above her eyes and head. She dare not move an inch.

There was no way of getting off the bed or reaching the call button without disturbing a web. The same for Vargas.

Megan shifted her eyes to the extreme right, pushing the

edges of her vision, trying to look at Vargas without moving her head. Trying to see if he was awake.

The pulse rate on his EKG machine read 130 beats per minute. And rising.

She shifted her eyes to the clock: 1:21 a.m.

No shift change until six . . . almost five more hours to go.

"Ricky," Megan whispered, tears filling her eyes. "DON'T MOVE."

ACKNOWLEDGMENTS

JAMES MURRAY

Firstly, thanks to my devilishly handsome cowriter and friend Darren Wearmouth. There's no one I'd rather spend Valentine's Day with than you . . . besides our wives, of course.

Thanks to Vikki Warner, Jeffrey Yamaguchi, Michael Carr, Kathryn Zentgraf, and the entire Blackstone team for their hard work and dedication to this project. Thanks to my colleagues and friends Joseph, Carsen, Nicole, Susan, Chá, and Ethan for their imagination and support. Thanks to Jack Rovner and Dexter Scott from Vector Management, Nick Nuciforo and Brandi Bowles from UTA, Danny Passman from GTRB, Phil Sarna and Mitch Pearlstein from PSBM, and Elena Stokes and team from Wunderkind PR. And special thanks to Brad Meltzer,

R. L. Stine, and James Rollins for your continued guidance and support on this journey.

Mom and Dad and my entire family, I love you all. Spear—I'll kill Liander in the next book, promise. And special thanks to my wife, Melyssa—by time you read this book, we'll be married, and I cannot imagine a better life than this.

And finally, thanks to all our amazing *Impractical Jokers* fans around the world for always believing in a few guys from Staten Island!

DARREN WEARMOUTH

James and I usually do a lot of our writing together. These are great times when we have lots of fun. He's a great host and a special guy. Unfortunately, all of our lives changed following the global pandemic. My family wasn't spared from its reach, and I know James has had family and friends affected as well. My heart goes out to any victim, family and friends, or those who have had their livelihoods taken. My faith in humanity convinces me that we'll bounce back stronger.

In light of the above, please forgive me for making personal acknowledgments. Thankfully, during lockdown, I've been with my great wife, Jennifer, and our beautiful daughter, Maple. We've stayed with her mother and father, Joe and Faye, and they've always been fantastic. I'd like to thank the staff at Blackstone who have been a pleasure to work with. Vikki Warner, our acquisitions editor and manager of the project. Michael Carr, our super helpful content editor. Kathryn Zentgraf, our eagle-eyed copy editor, and Jeffrey Yamaguchi, the head of marketing. Finally, a huge thank you to anyone who made it to this page of *Don't Move*. It's a story we loved creating and we are grateful that you've taken the time to read our work.